"Maybe we should get you checked out at the hospital."

"No! I just need to leave," Simone insisted.

"Okay, we can step outside," Lance offered.

"No, I mean leave Carling Lake."

The words hit him like a sucker punch. "What? Where would you go?"

"I don't know. I just have to get out of Carling Lake. I should have never moved back here."

"What did you mean you shouldn't have come back?"

"Nothing. I just really need to go."

"Why? I can't help feeling there's more to this than you're telling me."

The idea of Simone leaving Carling Lake and never seeing her again twisted his insides.

Several moments passed. She clearly knew something about his case. He had to press.

"Simone, you need to tell me what you meant. Someone broke in to your apartment. Left an obviously threatening message for you that appears to be connected to a murder. Let me help you."

After a long moment, she nodded. "Okay." She let out a deep breath. "I'll tell you everything."

CATCHING THE CARLING LAKE KILLER

K.D. RICHARDS

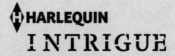

HHARLEQUIN®
INTRIGUE™

ISBN-13: 978-1-335-58256-0

Catching the Carling Lake Killer

For questions and comments about the quality of this book, please contact us at CustomerService@Harlequin.com.

Harlequin Enterprises ULC
22 Adelaide St. West, 41st Floor
Toronto, Ontario M5H 4E3, Canada
www.Harlequin.com

Printed in U.S.A.

Recycling programs for this product may not exist in your area.

K.D. Richards is a native of the Washington, DC, area, who now lives outside Toronto with her husband and two sons. You can find her at kdrichardsbooks.com.

Books by K.D. Richards

Harlequin Intrigue

West Investigations

Pursuit of the Truth
Missing at Christmas
Christmas Data Breach
Shielding Her Son
Dark Water Disappearance
Catching the Carling Lake Killer

Visit the Author Profile page at Harlequin.com.

CAST OF CHARACTERS

Lance Webb—Carling Lake sheriff.

Simone Jarrett—Staff reporter at the *Carling Lake Weekly*.

Erika West—B and B owner and Simone's friend; married to James West.

James West—Artist and gallery owner and works part-time for West Security and Investigations.

Melinda Hanes—Current mayor of Carling Lake, locked in a fierce election.

Aaron and Margaret Goodman—Owners and editors of the *Carling Lake Weekly*.

Zane Goodman—Website designer and Aaron and Margaret's son.

Kate Moretti—Intern at the *Carling Lake Weekly*.

Prologue

He hadn't planned on ever returning to his deadly pastime, but one never knows where life will take you. He'd met Holly and, well, he'd fallen back into some bad habits. And now he'd fallen back into another. He looked at the body in the grass at his feet.

Poor Holly. She shouldn't have threatened him. Pushy, demanding, aggressive women—he couldn't stand them. Women should know their place.

An anger he hadn't felt in years bubbled up inside of him like a newly awakened monster.

He'd managed to tamp the feeling down twenty years ago. To make it so small that he could pack it away in the recesses of his heart and mind and forget about it.

He'd had to if he didn't want to get caught.

But now, no one was looking for him. Carling Lake had all but forgotten about the Card Killer as the twentieth anniversary of the murders approached.

He'd killed Holly out of necessity, but maybe this was the hand of fate.

The monster inside of him stretched, breaking free

of the bindings he'd been relegated to for the past two decades.

Yes, maybe it was time for the Card Killer to make a return.

He reached into his wallet and pulled out the one memento he allowed himself from his prior kills. A card that he'd folded and kept inside his wallet for the past twenty years.

He unfolded it now and knelt, tucking it into the exterior pocket of the coat Holly wore before rising and turning his back on the body.

Yes, this felt right.

The Card Killer was back.

Chapter One

She ambled along the darkened street, the rumble in the sky warning of the imminent storm. But a little bit of rain seemed preferable at the moment to the argument raging back at the tiny house she shared with her mother and her mother's most recent boyfriend, Kyle. She was only twelve, but she'd been through the cycle enough times to know that the near constant arguing between Kyle and her mother meant that they'd soon be moving on from Carling Lake.

That was how it always went. Her mother hooked up with some guy and, for a while, things would be good. If the guy was nice, he might take them out for burgers or pizza a few times, maybe even buy her a trinket or two. But eventually, they'd start arguing. Not a lot at first, but the number and the ferocity of the arguments always increased—sometimes gradually, sometimes in what seemed like an instant. Her mother and the guy would break up, and in a few weeks, maybe a month, her mother would come home and declare she needed a fresh start. Then off they'd go to another new town. New house. New everything.

She hated it. Hated the arguments. Hated changing schools all the time. Hated never having any friends. Yamisha Jarrett could be vicious and say things that she was sure she shouldn't hear at her age. Her mother and Kyle were having one of those arguments right now, which was why she'd thrown the day's clothes back on and snuck out of the bedroom window. She didn't plan to stay out long. Just long enough for her mother, Kyle or both to storm out of the house.

She walked along the road that ran parallel to the woods separating the housing development where she lived from the nicer, newer one on the other side. Why did some kids have mothers who picked them up from school, made them home-cooked meals and went to parent-teacher conferences while she…didn't? She'd asked that question a thousand times in her short life. So far she hadn't gotten an answer.

Movement in the trees caught her eye. A woman drifted along the timeworn path that had developed as a result of the neighborhood residents cutting through the woods from one development to the next. The woman was some distance away lurching along on unsteady feet. She recognized the woman as one of the two who shared the house on the corner a block away from where she lived with her mother. It wasn't the first time she'd seen the woman stumbling home drunk.

Thunder clapped and fat drops of rain began to fall on her braided hair.

She pulled her hoodie up over her head and made

to turn away from the woman back toward her house when a man stepped from the shadows of the trees.

The woman froze.

So did she. A chill went through her, but it wasn't from the cold and rain.

The woman took a step backward, but the man reached out and grabbed her, dragging her toward him. The woman looked scared, as scared as she felt.

She ducked behind a tree, her chest rising and falling rapidly as if she'd just run several miles.

She didn't know who the man was, but instinct told her he planned to hurt the woman. She should run and get help. But fear kept her rooted to the spot.

The rain fell harder and faster now. She was already soaked through, and if the man and woman were saying anything at all, the storm made it impossible to hear it from where she was.

She peeked around the trunk of the tree.

The man wrapped something around the woman's throat—a rope? No, it was too thin to be a rope. A wire. He was strangling her!

Her heart pounded violently. She screamed for the man to stop, but the sound was whisked away by a sudden thunderclap.

The woman must have heard her or maybe she'd just sensed her there hiding among the trees. Their gazes met and the terror in the woman's eyes was palpable.

She thought about running at the man and striking him as hard as she could, but she was only twelve. If the woman couldn't fight him off, what chance did she have?

A second later the woman's eyes closed and she sagged in the man's arms.

He'd killed her. She'd just watched a woman die.

She had to get help now!

As if he felt her eyes on him, the man turned.

She didn't wait to see if he'd seen her. She darted through the trees, using them as cover as she ran back toward her house.

She had to get Momma. Kyle. They were adults. They'd know what to do.

She was almost there.

Then a figure stepped out of the darkness…

A ringing wrenched Simone Jarrett from the nightmare. Her first thought was that it was the gardeners that the building management contracted to mow the small patch of land running along the back of the building. They insisted on coming at ungodly hours and her complaints had so far been to no avail. The shrill sound came again and she woke up enough to realize it wasn't a lawn mower, but her cell phone.

"Hello," Simone croaked, rolling to her side.

"Reports of a dead body on the field behind the Watercress housing development." The voice of Aaron Goodman, co-owner and editor in chief of the *Carling Lake Weekly*, as well as her boss, boomed over the phone line.

She glanced at the clock—7:15 a.m.

"Simone, you there?"

She groaned but swung her feet onto the gray Berber carpeting that ran throughout her small apartment.

Her clothes from the day before conveniently lay hastily discarded on the bedroom floor. "I'm here."

A phone trilled on Aaron's end of the line. No surprise he was already in the office. "I'm texting you the address now."

"I've got an interview with Juanita Byers's sister Ernestine scheduled at ten this morning," she said, reminding him of the meeting that had taken her weeks to schedule.

Juanita Byers's death was one of three unsolved murders in Carling Lake. The twentieth anniversary of the most notorious crimes in the town's history was three weeks away and she'd convinced Aaron to let her pen a story commemorating the lives of the victims. At least that was how she'd sold the assignment to Aaron. What she hoped was that the story, and her digging, would shake loose new clues to the perpetrator's identity. The victims deserved justice after all these years.

And hopefully she'd find some redemption.

Before coming to Carling Lake, she'd worked at several middle-market newspapers on the hard news side, the last of which had been in Washington, DC. She'd seen all types of atrocities committed by man against his fellow man. But after nearly sixty years of covering area news, her former employer had succumbed to the fate of many other local newspapers and closed its doors. Her hunt for a new position had led her to discover that the *Carling Lake Weekly* was looking to hire a staff reporter.

She'd taken it as a sign. Living with what she'd

seen twenty years earlier and hadn't reported had been slowly eating away at her. Now, as the twentieth anniversary of the murder approached, here she was being given the opportunity to right the wrong. To go back and bring the Card Killer to justice.

"I'm sure you can handle both. Just get the story," Aaron said before ending the call.

As the only staff reporter at the *Carling Lake Weekly*, she covered everything. Aaron, and his wife and co-owner, Margaret, pitched in during the really busy times, but for the most part, she was it. Bake offs, break-ins, county council meetings, vandalism, the opening of a new superstore on Route 283, murder—she covered it all. With the Carling Lake mayoral race beginning to kick into high gear, she'd been working overtime covering the candidates' appearances and political events in addition to the regular local news. And for a small town, Carling Lake produced a lot of news.

She'd spent the previous night at incumbent mayor Melinda Hanes's fundraising event. Arriving home a little after 11:00 p.m., she'd been exhausted and ready to fall into bed. But when she'd opened the door to her apartment, she'd found a visitor who chased all thoughts of sleep from her mind. Sheriff Lance Webb. They had fallen into bed, spending the next few hours doing everything but sleeping.

Her eyes strayed to the empty bed now. The sheets were rumpled, an indentation still creasing the now vacant pillow, the faint scent of spicy aftershave hanging in the air. She wasn't surprised to find Lance had left before she'd awakened. In the weeks since they'd started whatever it was they'd been doing for the last two months now, Lance almost always left before sunrise. She was surprised, however, at the shock of disappointment she'd recently begun to feel when she didn't wake next to him.

"Casual. No strings." She reminded herself of the arrangement they'd struck after the first time they'd slept together. They'd agreed that they would both like to continue to see each other but that they needed guardrails. He was the town sheriff and she was a reporter. In a small town like Carling Lake, it was inevitable that there would be personal relationships that created conflicts of interest at times. But neither of them was keen to set the tongues of the town gossips wagging.

She got out of bed and started moving. After ten years of working as a professional reporter, she'd developed a system for getting dressed quickly. She started the coffee maker, then pulled her shoulder-length toffee-colored bob into a ponytail before hopping into the shower. Exactly six minutes later she got out, slathered lotion on her brown skin, pulled jeans over her curvy hips and donned a red sweater. Her low-heeled black leather boots were at the door where she'd kicked them off when she'd come in the night before. After double-checking to make sure she had the tools of her trade—notebook, laptop and cell phone—in her messenger bag, she made a quick stop in the kitchen to grab a coffee and she was on her way.

As a child, if an adult had ever bothered to ask her

what she wanted to be when she grew up, journalism probably would not have been on the list. She wasn't sure she would have had much of a list at all. Her mother hadn't been a shining example of responsibility or hard work, dragging her from town to town and picking up whatever odd jobs she could find, usually as someone's cleaning lady or waiting tables at the local greasy spoon. By the time Simone had hit her junior year in high school, she'd gone to nine different schools. Not exactly conducive to finding out what she truly wanted to do with her life. But the move in her junior year had come after the school year had already begun, which meant that she'd had to take whatever classes still had space at the new school, one of which had been a journalism elective. And the rest, as they say, is history. She'd somehow managed to find her calling among the chaos of her childhood. Or maybe despite it.

She slid into her gold 4Runner and headed for the address Aaron had texted her. Fifteen minutes later she arrived to find two police vehicles blocking the street in front of the large park behind the Watercress neighborhood. Television news vans from the two closest local stations were parked at the curb behind the police cruisers. Both stations covered a much wider geographical area than the *Carling Lake Weekly* and generally ignored the small town. The presence of the crews at the scene signaled the potential of a big story.

Now wide-awake and with adrenaline pumping, Simone parked on a side street two blocks away and hurried toward the small crowd of curious onlookers congregated around the perimeter the sheriff's department had set up.

The park was a large open area with a baseball field at the west end and a playground to the east. The cops had strung a tarp around a section of the field, blocking it from view of the street—a sure sign they had a body.

"Hey, Simone. Great piece on how the Carling Lake mayoral race is heating up," Eugene Ryan, the always perfectly coiffed on-air reporter from WRCW, said, flashing a smile as Simone approached the small crowd.

She returned his smile. "I knew you read my work."

"Mostly to see what not to do, but every once in a while you get it right," Eugene ribbed back.

She'd met Eugene soon after she'd joined the *Weekly*. At the time, a Carling Lake resident had just been arrested as part of a human smuggling ring and every news organization in a sixty-mile radius was covering the revelation nonstop. Aaron had thrown her into the deep end, assigning her to cover the investigations and subsequent trial of the culprits. Eugene had been covering the story for WRCW and they'd struck up a friendly, if somewhat competitive, working relationship. He was a damn good reporter and she hoped he thought the same of her.

She recognized the woman standing on the other side of Eugene as an on-air reporter for the WRCW's rival station, WKPT, but for the life of her she couldn't remember the reporter's name. It didn't seem to matter, since the woman's gaze was trained on the activity in front of her. She didn't so much as acknowledge Simone's or Eugene's presence.

"Did the sheriff give you anything yet?" she asked.

Eugene shook his head. "No, but here he comes."

Sheriff Lance Webb and Deputy Clark Bridges appeared around the side of the tarp and strode in their direction. For a moment the memory of him braced above her, his eyes dark with desire and lips plump from her kisses, flashed through her mind.

Eugene shot her a curious look. "You okay? You look a little flush."

She fanned her face with her hand. "Didn't have a chance to eat this morning." She made the excuse without looking at Eugene and kept her attention on the approaching lawmen.

"Are you investigating this case as a homicide?"

"Have you identified the victim?"

"Do you have any suspects?"

"Is the community safe?"

"The people who live here have a right to answers!"

The reporters and the residents lobbed questions faster than the sheriff could answer. Not that they were likely to get answers. Even if Lance had identified the victim, there was no way he would tell the press before notifying next of kin or while he was standing out in front of the crime scene. He might have been extremely creative in bed, but he was a by the book kind of guy when it came to the law.

She felt heat rush to her cheeks again until Lance swept a glare that could have turned water to ice over the small crowd. His eyes met hers briefly, but if he registered her presence any differently than the others, he didn't show it.

"I have a brief statement," he said, his tone making clear his unhappiness at having to address the group. "This morning at approximately six forty-five the sheriff's department received a call that an individual in the park needed medical assistance. The first unit to the scene confirmed that the person was deceased. I have no further information for you at this time."

"Should residents of this neighborhood be worried about their safety?" Simone shot her question at Lance as he and his deputy turned to walk away.

His gaze was chilly before, but now it shot flames. If he said nothing, the sheriff's department would be inundated with calls from nervous neighbors inquiring about what the police were doing to protect them and reporting every creak and groan in their houses. But if he answered, it would confirm that he didn't believe the crime was random.

"Everyone should always be aware of their surroundings and take necessary precautions to ensure their safety, but we do not have reason to believe the residents of the neighborhood are in any particular danger. I have nothing more for you at this time."

"How was the victim killed?" Simone pressed.

Lance turned a resolute gaze on her. "No. Comment."

She quelled the tingling building in her core. Despite herself, she found the stern lawman act very appealing.

The other two reporters shot several more questions at Lance as he retreated toward the crime scene.

Simone forced herself to focus on the job at hand and not the sexy lawman walking away. She turned to Eugene. "It's kind of weird, don't you think? You'd think the cops would want to put a neighborhood like this at ease."

Watercress was a mature, middle-class community with residents who were not used to and would not take lightly the discovery of a dead body on the field where their children played.

"The sheriff should have been itching to give us something to quell the masses. Have you heard anything else about who the possible victim could be?" she asked.

Eugene's eyes scanned over the scene. "No more than what you just heard. You gotta be one sick somebody to do this on a playground." He shook his head in disgust before ambling away toward his news van.

Simone couldn't disagree with that sentiment. But something didn't feel right about this. Lance was holding back, which wasn't in itself unusual. The cops never told the public everything. But why when it seemed like he'd want to put the community at ease as quickly as possible?

Simone scanned the small crowd of residents who still hung around. Two female joggers in yoga pants and parkas whispering to each other. A man in his early thirties with dark brown hair wearing a business suit, his phone attached to his ear. An older couple, the woman clutching the man's arm, while a white

Yorkie pranced and barked at the end of the leash he held in his other hand. It was a workday, but she was more than a little surprised the activity hadn't drawn more lookie-loos. Although, given the growing price tags on even the most modest homes in this neighborhood, the residents might have prioritized getting to work on time over rubbernecking.

She approached the group with a casual smile. "I'm a reporter with the *Carling Lake Weekly*. Do any of you know what's going on?"

The older woman clutched the man's arm tighter, looking Simone over as if she'd just demanded her purse. "We do not, and if we did, we certainly wouldn't talk to the press about it."

"Settle down, Hazel." One of the women in yoga pants stepped forward, rolling her eyes. "I'm Tansy Johnson. And she's Randa White." Tansy motioned to the other yoga pants–wearing woman. Randa looked decidedly less excited about talking to the press than Tansy, but she stepped up next to her friend. "We were jogging by when the police were setting up the tarp. I got a good look at the body on the ground. It was a woman." Excitement underlined Tansy's tone.

It wasn't much, but beggars couldn't be choosers. Simone glanced over her shoulder. The WKPT van was pulling away from the curb, but Eugene's van still idled. The last thing she wanted to do was to tip off the dogged reporter that she just might be getting the scoop, so while she itched to whip out her phone and start taking notes, she refrained for the moment. "Did you recognize her?"

Tansy's smile deflated. "No. And I didn't think to take a picture before the police got the tarp up."

"I don't think it's anyone who lives in the neighborhood." Randa's voice was high-pitched and sugary, more appropriate for a little girl than a grown woman.

"Why do you say that?" The sound of an engine had Simone shooting another look over her shoulder. The WRCW van was pulling away now. Great.

She slid her phone out of her pocket and opened the notes app.

"It's just that most of the people that live on this street, well, they have money." Randa leaned in and dropped her voice. "Like, real money."

Simone eyed the woman. "And you could tell the woman on the ground didn't have real money?"

Randa shook her head vehemently. "No way. I saw the coat she was wearing and it was…off-the-rack." Randa's nose crinkled as if she'd smelled something foul.

Simone assessed Randa's hundred-dollar Lululemon leggings, parka and running shoes that cost twice as much as the leather boots she was currently wearing. It figured a woman in a nearly five-hundred-dollar outfit just for jogging could probably identify "off the rack" from a mile away.

The older man stepped forward, dragging Hazel and his yappy dog with him. "I thought I heard a scream last night. Hazel said it was only the wind."

"Because it was the wind, Albert," Hazel admonished.

"Around what time did you hear the sound?" Simone asked, flashing a welcoming, keep-talking smile at Albert and ignoring Hazel.

"Oh, it must have been about eleven or so. I don't have a reason to go to bed early since I retired some years ago now. I like the late-night shows. I was watching the news, waiting for Colbert to come on when I heard the scream."

Simone pushed a little more, but the group had little else to add. They all agreed, even Hazel, that she could use what they'd said in her article, but none of them were willing to let her use their names.

She took out her phone and made notes of the conversation while Tansy and Randa resumed their jog and Albert and Hazel crossed the street and went into a colonial-style home with a black front door.

What she really needed was a look at what was happening behind the tarp.

Frowning, she scanned the street. The rear lawns of the houses one street over backed up to the park, wood-planked fences separating the private properties from the public grounds. A small window topped by a green roofline peeked over the top of one of the fences. A tree house.

She counted the number of homes from the end of the block to the one with the tree house, then hurried down the street away from the crime scene, hoping her exit wouldn't be noticed by the sheriff or his deputies. Once she'd rounded the corner, she broke into a slow jog until she got to the fourth house on the block.

She'd gone to questionable lengths before to get a

story, but she'd never knowingly broken the law. At least not a major law.

Her stomach churned. If she got caught spying on the crime scene from a child's tree house in a yard that wasn't hers, it would be impossible to explain away. She could be arrested for trespassing. As much as Aaron admired her drive to get the story at any cost, he couldn't be counted on for bail money.

For ten seconds she considered turning around and walking away.

Then the moment passed and she started up the path to the door of a white house with yellow shutters. The front yard was neat and carefully delineated with colorful flower beds. No car sat in the driveway, which boded well for what she planned to do.

She could hear the doorbell ring inside. Seconds passed, then a minute, and no one came to the door. She stepped off the small front porch and rounded the side of the house as if she belonged there.

A five-foot wooden fence lined the back of the property, but a waist-high chain-link fence wound around the other three sides. She lifted the metal latch on the fence and let herself into the backyard.

Where the front was well-kept, the backyard was clearly the kids' domain. Two bikes, one blue and one red, lay on the back patio. A soccer ball, basketball and baseball bat had been strewn across the yard, which was mostly dirt with patches of green trying to fight their way through.

The tree house was prefabricated and someone had nailed blocks of wood to the tree to create steps.

She shifted her messenger bag behind her and grabbed hold of the third block from the bottom. Fitting her thirty-two-year-old, five-foot-nine body through a hole and into a space designed for a small child took some navigating, but she finally made it to the window that faced the field, on her knees and hunched over.

The sheriff's department had only erected a tarp shielding the scene from the public street view, likely relying on the long, tall wood fencing that enclosed the yards that ran along the side of the playground. Most of the houses were ranch-styles, which would have made it difficult, if not impossible, to see the crime scene from a kitchen or bedroom window. But from the elevated tree house, she had a clear, if somewhat distant, view of the crime scene.

She twisted to reach into her bag, grateful that she'd splurged and gotten the top-of-the-line iPhone. The large screen and 10x zoom function were going to pay off in spades today.

She aimed the phone and zoomed in, snapping photos.

The body lay on its stomach on the wet sand of the baseball field. The victim was female, but she faced away from the neighboring backyards.

Simone's heart pinched.

There was a family out there somewhere wondering why their mother, daughter or sister hadn't come home last night. A family unprepared for the call they'd get, changing their lives forever.

The wind blew, rattling a loose board on the side of the tree house.

She focused on the man with a wild shock of silver hair jutting out to one side and wearing a windbreaker that read Medical Examiner across the back. He squatted next to the woman's body and looked up at Lance, who held a plastic evidence bag in his hand. There looked to be some sort of paper or card inside, but she was too far away to make out the writing on it.

She zoomed the phone's camera in on the bag and snapped a photo of the paper as her reporter's instincts began tingling. There was no way to be sure the homeowners wouldn't return home or that some nosy neighbor hadn't seen her go into the backyard. Spending too much more time on the property didn't seem wise.

But she couldn't stop herself from taking a moment to examine the picture on her phone more closely. There was something about the card in the bag Lance held. It looked…familiar.

She studied the photo for a moment, then gasped when the import of what she was looking at slid into place.

She was looking at a playing card, one with a unique design on one side that she'd seen before. It was a skull, with the word *pride* written across it in bloodred letters.

Her heart pounded and her breath came in labored gasps.

She'd seen a similar card twenty years ago and her life had never been the same.

Chapter Two

The rain from the night before had passed, but the late-October morning air remained crisp. Living in the mountains of New York meant he'd be pulling out his heavy winter coat sooner than he'd like, but for now Lance pulled the zipper on his windbreaker higher as he walked away from the small gaggle of reporters he'd felt forced to give a statement to. Murder always put him in a foul mood and having to deal with the press didn't help.

His gaze involuntarily tracked back toward the sidewalk where he'd given his press statement moments ago. He found the woman he sought talking to the crowd of neighbors now. He'd woken up feeling as if he was in heaven, lying next to a beautiful, sensual woman who challenged him in ways he couldn't have imagined before meeting her. And who he absolutely shouldn't be, but was, falling for. And then his phone rang.

His second-in-command, Deputy Clark Bridges, had responded to the initial call of a dead body in the Watercress neighborhood park and had already strung yellow police tape around the perimeter by the time Lance arrived. The park was adjacent to a residential street, which meant the police activity hadn't attracted as many onlookers as it might have downtown. Small favors.

Now he stood beside Deputy Bridges and the small circle of personnel about a quarter of the way into the field. An evidence tech took video while another snapped photographs. Medical examiner Scott Barber balanced on his haunches next to the body, a tech crouching next to him. In his early sixties with an untamable mop of white hair, Scott Barber reminded Lance of Christopher Lloyd's character in *Back to the Future*. And like Dr. Emmett Brown, Barber was a genius at what he did.

"Nasty business you got yourself into here, boys," Barber said without looking up from the body.

Lance couldn't disagree. He'd seen a lot of bodies in the years he'd spent first as part of the Atlanta Police Department and now as Carling Lake's sheriff. Overdoses. Hit-and-runs. Domestic abuse. Gunshots. Stabbings. Floaters surfacing after days underwater. So far it hadn't gotten any easier to deal with.

The woman lay on her stomach, her face turned to the side, her mouth open in a silent scream. Angry red lines circled her throat.

"Any idea who she is?" Bridges asked.

Barber looked up, shielding his eyes from the sun with a gloved hand. "Driver's license says Holly Moyer. There was also an employee identification card from the Fairmont Inn & Resort out on Route 283 with the same name. Pictures on both match the victim."

"What can you tell us now?" Lance asked.

Barber was a professional, he didn't like to speculate, but the faster Lance and his men got information, the more likely it was they'd catch whoever had done this.

"I haven't turned her over yet, but based on the marks on her neck, the likely cause of death is strangulation. Garroting, to be exact, since it appears that something, a thin piece of rope or wire, was used. I can tell you more about that when I get her back to my office."

A sense of unease swept over Lance. Garroting as a method for murder suggested premeditation and anger. A lot of anger.

He threw a glance at Bridges, who simply raised his eyebrows as Barber continued.

"You can see the marks there." Barber pointed to the space behind the body. "It looks like she was dragged or maybe fell. If she was already on her knees, it would have taken less effort to strangle her."

Barber motioned to his tech and together they rolled the victim onto her back. The forensic tech shifted position so he could record the medical examiner's actions.

"No other visible injuries," Barber said.

Lance studied the body. The woman's dark brown hair was matted, with grass and mud covering one side of her face as well as the front of her wool coat and tailored gray skirt suit. Her knees seemed to be particularly soiled, giving some heft to Barber's theory that she'd been on her knees at some point during the attack. Nothing else in the immediate vicinity gave any indication of what had led the woman to a deserted park in the middle of the night.

"The cell phone hers?" Lance asked, pointing to a black cell phone next to a yellow police marker with the number three on it.

"Yes, sir," one of the evidence techs, Nate Silver, answered. "It is password protected, but the photograph on the lock screen is of our victim."

"Did the killer miss the cell phone or was he not interested in it?" Lance asked more to himself than to anyone standing nearby.

"Her wallet was in her purse, found over there." Bridges pointed to a spot twenty yards away. A black leather purse lay on its side next to another evidence marker. "Money, credit cards and car keys still inside the wallet."

"So not a robbery," Lance said, feeling the skin on his forehead furrow. "Have we found the car?"

Bridges shook his head. "Keys are for a BMW, but there isn't one in the parking lot that we've found. Maybe she walked?"

"Maybe. But why?" Another possibility was that she'd been driven to the park by her killer.

"Barber, you got an estimated time of death?" Lance asked.

Barber stood. "Between ten last night and six this morning. I should be able to narrow it down for you by this evening."

Lance turned back to Deputy Bridges. "Where are the kids who found her?"

He hated that it was teenagers who had stumbled across the body.

"I've got them sitting in a cruiser." Bridges pointed to where his sheriff's cruiser sat at the end of the block. "They were cutting through the park on the way to school and found the body."

"We'll talk to them next," Lance said, looking to Bridges for confirmation.

Bridges nodded.

He'd need to assign at least one more deputy in addition to Bridges to canvass the neighborhood for the woman's vehicle and to learn if any of the residents had seen anything out of the ordinary. Maybe they'd get lucky and someone's home security camera had caught a visual of the woman with her killer.

He and Bridges left Barber to oversee the removal of the body and headed for where the kids who'd made the gruesome morning discovery waited.

Lance scanned the diminishing crowd as he walked toward the sidewalk and the cruiser. The small gathering of people along with the handful of reporters had dispersed. Could one of the people watching in their business suits or yoga pants be the killer? If Barber was right about the woman having been on her knees when she was killed, almost anyone, even a teenager, could have been strong enough to make the kill quickly.

He turned his attention to the two boys unfolding from Deputy Bridges's vehicle. They were both in the gangly awkward stage of adolescence. One was white with a long face and a shock of red hair the color of cranberries. The other was Black, stood nearly half a foot taller than his friend and sported shoulder-length dreadlocks.

"Hi, guys. I'm Sheriff Webb and this is Deputy Bridges. Can you tell us your names?"

The redhead eyed them wearily but gave his name as Gabriel Moses. His friend was Daniel Green.

"We just want to ask you a few questions, okay?" Lance said.

"We're already late for school," Gabriel replied testily.

Lance narrowed his eyes at the redhead. Interviewing kids took a delicate balance of diplomacy and patience that Bridges, with a preteen son at home, was far more adept at exercising than he was.

"We let the school know you were helping us out this morning," Bridges said. "You won't be in any trouble and I'll have someone take you to school in just a minute."

"Can you tell us how you came upon the woman in the park?" Lance asked, earning a look from Bridges.

"We were just cutting through like we always do," Gabriel shot out. "And she was just lying there. Dead."

"The park is the fastest way. Otherwise, we'd have to walk around and that'll add five extra minutes." Daniel bit his bottom lip, worry clouding his eyes.

Bridges smiled at the teens. "You all aren't in any

trouble. We just need to know if you saw anybody around on your way to school this morning."

"No. Just the same as always. A couple of people in a rush to get to work and a guy walking a dog. Don't know 'em though." Gabriel picked at the cuff of his jacket sleeve.

"How about you, Daniel? See anyone unusual or anything out of place?"

Daniel shook his head.

Lance pulled two business cards from his coat pocket. "Okay, boys. Deputy Bridges is going to take you to school now. If you remember anything at all, please give one of us a call." Lance handed over the business cards and Bridges did the same.

The boys stuffed them into their pockets without looking and climbed back into the car.

Lance motioned for Bridges to follow and stepped several feet away to ensure the boys couldn't overhear them. "Take the boys to school, then pull Deputy Page and canvass the neighborhood for the BMW and for anyone that might have seen something suspicious last night or this morning."

"Got it." Bridges headed for the cruiser but stopped when a whistle drew both their attention back to the field.

"I've got something for you, Sheriff," Barber called.

"Get the boys to school. I'll update you when you get back," Lance said to Bridges, already heading for Barber.

"Found this in the front pocket of her coat." Barber handed him a plastic evidence bag when Lance rejoined him at the center of the crime scene.

Lance's heart lurched into his throat. He'd seen photographs of similar playing cards in the file for Carling Lake's three unsolved murders.

"I don't know how familiar you are with—" Barber started.

"I'm familiar," Lance interrupted.

A skull with the word *pride* was drawn on the back of the playing card.

Barber pinned Lance with his dark blue eyes. "If you recognize this card, I'm sure I don't have to tell you that this case has the potential to implode this town."

"I know, Barber, I know."

Lance sighed. That was an understatement. If the Card Killer was back and killing again after twenty years, there was no telling how residents would react.

Unease swept through him.

Something shifted in the tree house perched in one of the backyards that lined the perimeter of the field. He strained to see, then realizing what he was looking at, he felt a surge of annoyance.

"Make sure this gets back to the station with all the other evidence," he said, handing the card off to Barber before marching away from the crime scene.

He caught up with Simone at her car.

She unlocked the driver's-side door and reached for the handle. He shot his hand out, keeping her from opening the door.

"Want to tell me what you were doing spying on my crime scene from a tree house?"

"I have no idea what you're talking about, Sheriff." Her lips curved upward in what he took as an attempt to smile, but it didn't mask the anxiety in her eyes. Her breath came quickly, and her face was flushed, possibly because she'd been moving fast to get down out of that tree house and back to her car, but he didn't think that was all there was to it.

His gut clenched with anxiety. "What's wrong?"

"Nothing's wrong," she said, her gaze skittering away from him. She was lying. "But I do need to get to the office, so if you don't mind." She gestured to the hand he was using to keep her from opening her car door.

He moved closer to her, the desire to wrap her in his arms powerful, but he resisted the public show of affection. They'd been sleeping together for two months now, more than enough time for him to get a feel for when something was off with her, even if he hadn't been a trained investigator. "Hey, you can talk to me, you know."

Her gaze finally found his and want flushed through him. Thoughts of the activities they'd been engaged in a few hours earlier flickered through his mind as did the desire to do it all over again.

He was getting in too deep. Hell, he was already in too deep. Theirs was supposed to be a causal relationship built solely around mutual attraction and desire. But he'd realized a few weeks ago that somewhere along the way he'd developed feelings far beyond the casual.

Which was a problem. First, Simone had been very clear that she was not looking for a relationship. And second, their respective careers would make a real relationship difficult.

But not impossible.

Not impossible. Neither of their employers had policies prohibiting their relationship, but it was bound to raise eyebrows around town.

So? Anything worth having was worth fighting for.

And he had a growing feeling that Simone Jarrett was worth fighting for.

He removed his hand from the car and cupped her face. "You can trust me."

She pressed her cheek into the palm of his hand for a moment before stepping back, her expression guarded. "Lance, I have to go."

She was definitely keeping something from him, but pushing her on it wouldn't get him anywhere.

He stepped away from the car. "Stay out of tree houses. I'd hate to have to arrest you for breaking and entering."

She tried to smile, but it fell short.

For the second time in the last ten minutes, unease rolled through him as he watched her drive away.

Chapter Three

Simone entered the building that housed the *Carling Lake Weekly*'s headquarters but veered off for the ladies' room before heading to Aaron's office. She knew he'd want to know what she had on the story ASAP, but her mind was still reeling.

She pulled up short just inside the bathroom door.

Kate Morelli, the *Weekly*'s postgraduate intern, was washing her hands at the bathroom sink.

"Everything okay, Simone?" Kate shut off the faucet and pulled a paper towel from the dispenser on the wall.

"Yes, fine." She forced a smile.

"Okay, well, Aaron asked me to help you with whatever research you need on the story from this morning." Kate dropped her voice reverently. "You know, the body that was found."

Simone felt her smile drop into a frown. It wasn't that she didn't like Kate. She did. The young woman was bright and a hard worker. She had graduated summa cum laude with a journalism degree from Stony Brook. But Simone preferred working alone.

Research could be time-consuming, but doing it herself allowed her to put her thoughts together coherently. However, Aaron had been keen on the new internship program he'd started and had looked for work for Kate everywhere he could find it.

"Well, let's talk later, okay? I'm not sure what I'll have for you to do."

Kate nodded, but her smile had turned into a frown now as well. She hurried from the restroom, leaving Simone to concentrate on the thoughts that had driven her to seek solitude in the ladies' room in the first place.

Over a period of three weeks twenty years ago, the bodies of three women had been found strangled: Deborah Indigo, Juanita Byers and Nancy Oliver. Each of the women had also been found with a card the size of a playing card on her body. Only these cards hadn't been for poker or blackjack. They were specially designed with a skull on one side and one of several vices written in red marker on top. Deborah's card had read Lust, Juanita's Greed and Nancy's Gluttony. Because of the cards, the killer had been dubbed the Card Killer.

Nancy Oliver. The woman and her murder had haunted Simone every day for twenty years.

Watching Nancy get murdered, and running away, had left a wound so deep she wasn't sure it would ever heal. But she hoped identifying the killer might start the process. It was why she'd returned to Carling Lake six months ago. And why she'd hounded

Aaron until he'd given in and let her write a story about the murders.

Simone pictured the multiple files of notes, clippings and reports she had stored away on the cloud as well as on the backup flash drive that was hidden in the American Heart Association wristband she wore. She'd donated both her time and money to the association's various fundraisers and awareness campaigns ever since her mother's fatal heart attack at the shockingly young age of forty. The wristband-slash-flash-drive was one of the trinkets given away to donors or volunteers at an event Simone couldn't even remember.

The former Carling Lake sheriff, Matt Reeser, had called in a state police profiler. She hadn't been able to obtain a copy of the original profile; her sources didn't extend that far. But from what she had been able to gather, the profile pegged the killer as a male somewhere between the ages of twenty and thirty-five, familiar with Carling Lake and the surrounding area, possibly a resident or frequent visitor with the usual abnormal home life, tough upbringing and difficulty relating to others. Since the cards left with the bodies listed well-known vices, the profiler speculated that the killer might have been motivated to kill people he felt had somehow transgressed against his moral code. All three victims had been women, so chances were a woman close to him exemplified one or more of these vices in his mind. The profiler felt that the killer's first victim might have been someone close to him, but no one close to Deborah Indigo was ever identified as a suspect. Which begged the question: Was Deborah really the killer's first victim or just the first the authorities knew about?

Despite a massive effort by the sheriff's department, they'd never found enough evidence to identify a suspect or even a person of interest. And after the third murder, the killing had abruptly stopped. No one was sure why, but after a time it seemed as if Carling Lake had just forgotten about the murders and moved on.

Was it possible the Card Killer had started killing again?

Maybe he'd never stopped. The killer could have moved on, to a bigger city possibly where there was a larger pool of victims and his crimes were more likely to go undetected. Then why come back to Carling Lake after all this time and pick up where he'd left off?

Simone took a deep breath, the voice in her head urging her to slow down.

One of the biggest mistakes a reporter could make in pursuing a story was jumping to conclusions. Instincts and gut feelings had their place, but only the facts mattered.

And right now the only fact she had was that a card that looked similar to ones found in connection with three twenty-year-old murders had been found at this morning's crime scene. She needed more. And until she had it, she wasn't going to tell Aaron about the card or her connection to Nancy Oliver's murder.

She withdrew her cell phone from her handbag and

sent the photos she'd taken at the morning's crime scene to her cloud account before deleting the ones that showed the playing card from the phone.

She knew not telling Aaron was walking right up to, if not hopping right over, a professional line, but this was one story she was willing to risk her career and reputation for. Nancy, Juanita and Deborah deserved justice and she intended to see that they got it.

She left the bathroom and headed for Aaron's office. She wasn't surprised to find his son, Zane, sitting there when she arrived.

Aaron's eyes lit up when she entered. She recognized the thirst for a juicy story in them.

"What do you have for me?" he demanded.

She gave him the rundown. Female found, deceased, on the playground field behind the Watercress neighborhood. No name for the victim, but the neighbors seemed to think she didn't live in the neighborhood.

"One neighbor might have heard a scream last night around eleven," she said. She showed him and Zane the photos of the crime scene she'd left on her phone.

"So it's a homicide?" Aaron asked, swiping through the photos.

"The sheriff didn't confirm that, but what else could it be? Women don't just fall dead in parks in the middle of the night."

Aaron glanced up. "We can't call it a homicide without confirmation. Write it up as a suspicious death for now. There are a few good shots there." He handed the phone back to her. "Of course, we can't use the ones of the actual body in the paper. I don't want to even know how you got those, but good work. Did the sheriff make a statement?"

Simone made a face. "A lot of words that amounted to no comment."

"This has a bad déjà vu feeling to it." A visible shudder shook Zane's body as he spoke.

Simone studied her boss's son. She wouldn't exactly categorize Zane as a coworker. From the few conversations they'd had, she'd learned that he had worked at the *Weekly* as an intern while taking a gap year between high school and college. But Zane's heart hadn't been in journalism. When he had finally gone off to college, he'd studied computer engineering. After years of working in New York City as a web designer, he'd decided he could make just as much money and have a better quality of life striking out on his own as a freelance web designer and moving back to Carling Lake. He'd arrived a month after she'd started at the *Weekly* and pretty much worked out of the conference room at the paper ever since.

For a while, after Zane moved back and set up shop at the *Weekly*, she'd wondered if he had decided to take another stab at journalism and was gunning for her job. But Zane seemed happy designing web pages and logos for his clients all over the country. They'd settled into a familiar, if somewhat awkward, friendship.

"Déjà vu?"

Zane's gray eyes cut across the small office to her. "I guess déjà vu isn't the right term. I just meant that

Carling Lake doesn't have a lot of crime. Especially not murders. But lately...there was that young woman found out at Lakewood House and now this woman."

A young woman had been found dead on a property next to the lake several months ago. She'd been kidnapped by human traffickers who Lance had caught and arrested. Simone hadn't been with the *Weekly* for the arrests, but she'd written several articles on the subsequent trial and conviction of the perpetrators.

"And everybody is already on edge with the twentieth anniversary of the Card Killer murders coming up." Zane glanced at his father.

Aaron ran a hand through his thinning hair and frowned. "I know. Simone is doing a story on the murders. A look at where the investigation stands after all these years and questioning whether the killer will ever be caught."

It had taken a bit of convincing to get him on board with letting her write the article. He hadn't been sure that rehashing the past was good for the town.

"Twenty years ago you would have been working at the *Weekly*, right? I think I saw your byline on one of the articles."

Zane picked at his cuticle, looking uncomfortable. "I wrote a story or two, but I wasn't good at writing the hard-hitting stuff."

"Zane mostly stuck to writing the feel-good pieces and keeping the public abreast of the goings-on at the town council and school board meetings," Aaron chimed in.

Zane smiled weakly. "I told you, I wasn't cut out to be a journalist. Especially not to report on the nastier side of society."

Simone looked at the clock on Aaron's wall. It was almost nine thirty. "I have that interview with Ernestine Parks at ten." She headed for the office door. "I'll shoot you enough to go up on the website before I leave for the interview."

"Okay, but, Simone…?" The edge to Aaron's voice stopped her before she left the office. She turned back to him. "I know it's still early days with this investigation, but this morning's body takes precedence over the anniversary piece. Use Kate for research, calls, whatever. You'll need help. What's happening now is what our readers care about and what sells papers."

The idea that she'd need help with her story rankled, but she nodded and left Aaron's office. She didn't have time for ego or office politics. Not when there was a possibility that a serial killer was stalking the streets of Carling Lake again.

Chapter Four

Lance looked at the files on his desk. Three yellow folders, each one representing a woman who had fallen victim to the Card Killer twenty years ago. A killer who might be killing again.

That was what he was determined to find out. Was Holly Moyer a victim of the same man who'd killed Nancy Oliver, Deborah Indigo and Juanita Byers twenty years ago? Or did they have a copycat? Or was Holly's killer simply trying to send investigators on a wild-goose chase? Most murder victims, after all, are killed by someone they knew and trusted.

He hated informing people of loss over the phone, but Holly's parents were her next of kin and they lived in Seattle. They'd been devastated by the news of her death. They also hadn't been able to give him much helpful information. Holly had graduated from a small college in Vermont with a degree in hospitality management. She'd decided to stay on the East Coast when she'd gotten the job at the Fairmont. They didn't know who her friends were and she hadn't mentioned dating anyone.

He didn't even know why Holly was in Carling Lake. The address on her driver's license was in Stunnersville. The three victims from years ago had all lived in Carling Lake. Was killing Holly here some sort of message from the killer? Or had Holly just been a victim of opportunity?

They'd found her car on a residential street in the Watercress neighborhood not far from the field where they'd found and processed the body. Barber thought the case had the potential to implode the town and Lance couldn't disagree. He planned to do everything he could to make sure that didn't happen.

Carling Lake had given him more than he could ever give back to the town. A place to regroup when life had kicked him in the teeth. A job. Good friends. A home. To say he was protective of the town and the residents was an understatement.

Especially one gorgeous, albeit secretive, new resident, the little voice in his head teased.

Simone was a strong, intelligent woman, but she had firmly erected emotional walls. And he didn't think it was just because they'd agreed to keep their relationship casual. She was hiding something. Something that seemed to be eating away at her. Everything in him wanted to ease that burden for her.

He shook his head to clear it of thoughts of Simone. He needed to focus. He opened the file on top of the pile and began to read even though he'd committed every piece of information in these folders to memory years earlier.

The three women killed years ago had all been Carling Lake residents, but outside of that they had little in common. Deborah, the first victim, was a fifty-two-year-old housewife, recent empty nester and regular volunteer at her church. The former sheriff, Reeser, had looked hard at her husband, but he'd had a rock-solid alibi and no motive. Neither had anyone else in Deborah's life. Reeser hadn't known what to make of the card with the skull with the word *lust* written across it.

Two weeks after Deborah's murder, Juanita Byers's body had been discovered. Juanita was thirty-three, a loving mother and wife with a stable job. Her husband's background was complicated, but he, like Deborah's husband, had a solid alibi. Floyd Byers had been serving thirty days in the local county jail for passing a bad check. The discovery of a card similar to the one they'd found with Deborah's body, but with the word *greed*, raised the fear that they were dealing with a serial killer.

The third victim, Nancy Oliver, was a twenty-year-old troubled young woman who'd had a number of minor run-ins with the law. The card found with her body read Gluttony. Three women from different socioeconomic backgrounds, different races and different ages had all somehow caught the eye of a killer who'd been smart enough to elude authorities for two decades.

He looked over the files in front of him. There had

to be something in these files that could at least help him identify a suspect.

A knock at the door pulled his attention from his work.

Deputy Clark Bridges stood in the doorway. "Canvassing is done. I'll get the report to you by close of business, but the long and short of it is we got nothing."

"How is that possible? All those homes and none of them had security cameras that picked up anything?"

Bridges shook his head. "None of the security cameras extend to the park and the security camera footage we've gotten doesn't show our victim or anyone else suspicious."

Unsurprised, he let out a heavy sigh. The killer was far too smart to be so easily identified. "Okay. Let's make sure we've talked to all the neighbors." He looked at his watch. "I'm going to head over to the ME's office. See if Barber has found anything that will point us in the right direction."

Bridges glanced over his shoulder. His eyebrows rose as he stepped away from the door. "Ah, you might have to wait on that, boss. The mayor is headed your way."

Lance rose from his chair and greeted Mayor Melinda Hanes as she strode into his office. "Mayor Hanes."

"Sheriff Webb."

Melinda Hanes had not been a fan of his since he'd arrested her brother a year earlier on illegal gambling, corruption and fraud charges. Their tenuous working relationship had been further strained when his friend Nikki King jumped into the upcoming mayoral race.

Melinda set her purse on the visitor chair but remained standing.

"What can I do for you, Madam Mayor?"

"I'd like to know where you stand with the investigation into the body found this morning."

"Well, as you know, we only discovered the victim this morning. We've identified the victim and spoken to her next of kin. I've got men canvassing the area around the crime scene and I was just about to go to the medical examiner's office."

"I'm sure I don't have to tell you that a crime like this, a murder, mustn't go unpunished."

"Of course not."

"I know you aren't from Carling Lake." She lifted her chin. "But you must be aware of the town's most notorious and only unsolved crimes."

"Of course."

"The media dubbed the murderer the Card Killer and ran wild with the serial killer in a small town story. I was little more than a child, but I remember the fear that wracked the residents. To say nothing of the economic damage that it caused. It took years for Carling Lake to recover fully."

"We don't know that this murder has anything to do with the Card Killer, but if the investigation leads us down that path, I will pursue it."

"But you did find a card with a skull emblem on it, correct?"

He'd planned to hold the information about the card

back, but if the mayor knew about it, chances were others knew about it too. His blood boiled at the idea that someone in his department might have leaked information. "Yes, but as I said, we are still in the early days of our investigation."

"I do not plan to let this town fall prey to the media's thirst for a juicy story this time. I think it would be best if you found the perpetrator of this heinous crime quickly and kept any and all talk about the Card Killer or serial killers under wraps."

"As I said, I will go where the evidence leads," he gritted out between clenched teeth.

Melinda's eyes narrowed into slits. "I know you're hoping your friend unseats me in the upcoming mayoral election. If you think I'm just going to let you twist this murder so that Nikki King can use it against me, you have another thing coming."

He felt the muscles in his back tense and his jaw harden. "Mayor, all I care about is finding the person or persons who killed Holly Moyer and I will do that the best way I see fit regardless of how it may affect your reelection."

Her lips tightened into a thin line. She glared across the desk at him for several long moments before picking up her purse and turning away. She made it to the office door, then turned back. "I'm not someone you want to have as an enemy, Sheriff."

"Neither am I, Madam Mayor."

Chapter Five

Simone parallel parked in front of a redbrick house atop a steep incline. Ernestine Parks was the sister of the second victim of the Card Killer. She'd seemed surprised when Simone reached out to her, but she'd agreed to an interview in the hopes of reigniting attention to her sister's murder. It had been twenty years, but Ernestine had never given up hope that her older sister's murderer would be caught.

Not every journalist was cut out for the task of speaking with bereaved loved ones. Many were uncomfortable prying into the personal lives of a victim. Others only saw the story through a professional sense—what a sensational story might do for their careers. Those stories tended to be exploitative and drew the ire of family members and the community. Of course, those were the stories editors secretly loved—the stories that got clicks, were retweeted and trended on social media.

To Simone, the profile piece encapsulated what journalism, in its purest form, was all about. Exposing the emotion—the love, hurt, pain and passion—of the people behind the story. Bringing a little human-ity to all the chaos in the world.

She couldn't bring Juanita or the other women back, but she could memorialize their lives and make sure they weren't forgotten. And maybe, just maybe, her profile would also jog a memory or move someone to finally go to the police with information.

Simone climbed the porch stairs and rang the door-bell. It chimed and a moment later the door swung open to reveal an African American woman with sad eyes and a kind smile.

"Ms. Parks? I'm Simone Jarrett."

"Yes, of course. Come in, please." Ernestine opened the door wider and stepped aside so Simone could pass.

A gale of Jean Nate assaulted her olfactory nerves as Ernestine closed and bolted the door before lead-ing the way farther into the house.

Like many of the older homes in town, the rooms were smaller and more closed off than the newer houses that seemed to be springing up in Carling Lake these days.

Ernestine turned left at the end of a short hall into a living room with an oversized floral couch in faded shades of pink and green. Matching high-backed arm-chairs sat opposite the couch, the two seating options separated by a sturdy wooden coffee table. A tea set and plate with an assortment of cookies waited on the table.

Ernestine waved Simone to one end of the couch before settling at the other end.

"Would you like tea? I made the sugar cookies myself." She nodded toward the plate on the table.

"Thank you." Simone took a cookie, placing it on top of her open notebook and hoping the ink from her pen didn't rub off onto the cookie. Ernestine poured two cups of tea and slid one toward Simone before balancing the other on her lap.

"I want to say again how sorry I am for your loss," Simone said.

Ernestine dipped her head with the graciousness of a queen. "Thank you. Even after all these years, whenever we get close to the day..." She paused, seemingly willing the tears welling in her eyes not to fall. "Well, it hasn't gotten any easier." Ernestine took a tissue from the cuff of her sleeve and dabbed her eyes.

"I'm hoping the article will show people how kind and dedicated to the Carling Lake community Juanita was and maybe jog some memories about the days surrounding her murder."

"That would be good. I've never stopped praying for my sister's killer to be found." Ernestine sat up straighter and pushed her tissue back into her sleeve. "Juanita was very active in the community, especially her church."

Simone took notes as Ernestine described her sister's life. Although Ernestine was now in her fifties, her voice still carried a whisper of younger sister idolization when she spoke about her older sister. Simone already knew the details of Juanita's life and murder, but she listened patiently as Ernestine described her sister's too-short life.

Juanita Byers had been born and raised in Carling Lake, one of two children to parents who both worked at the then nearby auto manufacturing plant. An intelligent, pragmatic and focused woman, Juanita had put off dating seriously until she'd obtained her associate degree in program management and established her career as a top-notch executive assistant. When she'd finally fallen in love, she'd fallen hard.

As a town reliant on tourism, Carling Lake was used to its fair share of seasonal workers passing through. Floyd Byers rolled into town looking for work during the Spring Festival and found Juanita.

"Nita didn't know it then, but a good part of why Floyd moved to Carling Lake was because he had every loan shark between the Mississippi River and the Chesapeake Bay chasing him. The law too, we came to find out later." Ernestine shook her head, disgust still ringing in her tone.

She took a long sip of tea before picking up Juanita's life story.

"Four months after meeting Floyd, Juanita discovered she was pregnant. At first, she and Floyd had been over the moon. Nita already owned this home and Floyd just moved right in." Ernestine frowned. "At least he had the decency to marry my sister first. But what Floyd couldn't seem to do was get and keep a decent job. But Nita would hear no criticism of Floyd. She paid all the bills and, after the baby came, did most of the parenting too. 'Course she didn't have much choice after a while. It didn't take Floyd long to start catting around. Nita put up with it for a while, but by the time Brian Jacob—Nita and Floyd's son, —turned five, she'd had enough. She kicked Floyd out and filed for divorce. Although I will say, I don't think Nita ever stopped loving that man."

"So Floyd wasn't living here at the time Juanita was killed?"

Ernestine shook her head. "No. He and Nita had been divorced about a year by that time. Didn't stop Sheriff Reeser from looking at him hard though."

"Do you know if the sheriff had a specific reason for pressing Floyd or was it just because he was the ex?"

Ernestine sniffled. "Floyd had a temper. Nita said he never touched her or Brian, but I had my suspicions. I saw the bruises. Nita always had an excuse, but I didn't believe her. I told the sheriff about them after Nita's murder. That could have had something to do with why they pressed Floyd so hard. But there was that other woman who'd been murdered so much like Nita."

"Deborah Indigo. Did Juanita or Floyd know her?"

Ernestine shrugged. "Floyd? Who knows? But Nita, I remember her being shocked that a murder like that would happen here in Carling Lake. I'm sure if she knew the woman, she would have told me."

Connection between Nita, Floyd, Deb? Simone scribbled in her notebook.

"Do you know where Floyd is now?" Simone asked.

"Heavenly Angels Cemetery. He died of lung cancer about ten years ago now."

Which meant even if Floyd was the Card Killer, he couldn't have killed the woman found this morning.

"I'm sorry to hear that."

Ernestine nodded her appreciation for the sentiment. "Brian took it hard. Whatever his father's faults, that boy loved him unconditionally. I took over guardianship of him after Nita's death, since Floyd had never had an interest in being a full-time father. My parents were older and didn't have the energy to take on an active six-year-old. I raised Brian just as I would have my own child if I'd ever been so blessed."

"I'm sure you did a wonderful job." With her research into Juanita's life and family, she knew Brian was a mechanic at a nearby auto body shop.

Simone took a nibble of her cookie, contemplating how to bring up what was likely to be a sensitive subject. It was never easy to delve into the specifics of the circumstances that might have led to a loved one's death, but it had to be done.

"I'm sure you know about the card that was with your sister."

Ernestine made a face as if she'd smelled something foul. "Yes, that skull business. The sheriff confirmed it after you folks in the media reported it."

As was the case with the body found earlier that morning, the sheriff's office had attempted to hold back the information about the playing cards twenty years ago, but it was pretty difficult to keep a salacious detail like that from leaking.

"The card had the word *greed* written on it. Do you have any idea why?"

Ernestine sighed heavily and leaned forward, sliding her teacup and saucer onto the coffee table. "Juanita had lost her job at the pharmacy a few weeks before she was taken from us. The owner, Harry Wright, accused her of stealing from the register."

Harry Wright still owned the pharmacy. Simone made a note to speak to him.

Ernestine's eyes turned hard. "She hadn't stolen anything of course. Juanita would never do such a thing, but Wright wouldn't listen to her. To this day I refuse to have my prescriptions sent to his pharmacy. He had the nerve to send flowers for Juanita's funeral after his lies cost her job and made her the talk of the town gossips."

And it may have put her on the radar of a killer if the profiler's theory about how the killer picked his targets was correct.

Heavy footsteps sounded on the front porch. Ernestine leaned to the side and looked through the large picture window at Simone's back. Simone swiveled on the sofa but couldn't see the person who'd stepped onto the porch.

"That's Brian now. He comes over every day to check on me. I took a little spill a few months back and now he wants me to move into an adult-centered community." She made air quotes around the last three words and rolled her eyes. "Can you believe it? I'm only fifty-two!"

Simone smiled at the woman as the front door

opened then closed and the sound of footsteps carried toward them.

"Aunt Ernie? Whose car is that parked in front of the house?" A stout man with dreadlocks that swept his shoulders, wearing a green jacket, blue work coveralls and work boots, stepped into the living room. He smiled at his aunt, but the smile fell from his face when his gaze fell on Simone. "Who are you?"

"Brian! That's no way to speak to my guest," Ernestine said.

Brian's frown only deepened.

Simone stood and offered her hand. "My name is Simone Jarrett. I'm with the *Carling Lake Weekly.*"

Brian ignored her hand, his eyes swinging back to his aunt. "I thought we agreed you were going to cancel the interview with the reporter. I told you they just want to sensationalize Mama and those other women's deaths so people will buy more papers."

The tension in the air was nearly tangible. Simone slid her notebook into her messenger bag. "That's really not my intention."

"I don't care nothing about your intentions," Brian said bluntly, glowering.

Ernestine pushed up from her seat now too. "Brian, Ms. Jarrett's article just might jog someone's memory or induce them to go to the sheriff with some evidence that could lead to your mother's killer. If the paper gets a few new subscriptions, that's more than a fair trade-off for me."

Brian's hands curled into fists at his sides. He made

a low sound in his throat. "Not to me." He glowered at Simone. "I'd like for you to leave."

Ernestine was a few inches shorter than her nephew, but she appeared to instantly grow the inches she needed to meet his gaze head-on. "This is not your house, young man."

The dark expression on Brian's face set Simone's stomach knotting. "It's okay, Ms. Parks. I believe I have everything I need."

Ernestine Parks glowered at her nephew for several more seconds. "Let me show you out."

The older woman moved toward the entrance to the living room, forcing Brian to step aside as she marched into the hall. She held the front door open as Simone stepped out onto the porch.

"Please forgive my nephew," she said, her voice pitched low. "As I said, this time of year is very difficult for us. Brian doesn't handle it well at all, I'm afraid."

Simone smiled reassuringly at the woman. "It's okay. You take care of yourself."

Movement over Ernestine's shoulder caught Simone's eye as the door closed. Brian stood in the hallway several feet behind his aunt, his dark eyes narrowed into menacing slits.

Brian Byers was a young man bubbling over with anger. Was it possible that anger had turned him into the same kind of monster that had taken his mother from him?

Chapter Six

Lance stood in Holly Moyer's light-filled office with Fred Knauer, the manager of the Fairmont Inn & Resort. The manager was jittery, which wasn't out of the ordinary. Many people were nervous talking to the police, sometimes because they were hiding something, but for others, just the presence of law enforcement was enough to set them on edge.

Lance wasn't sure which category Fred Knauer fell into. Maybe neither. It was also quite possible that Knauer's nerves were a result of the gin Lance smelled on his breath when he'd introduced himself to the man. And it wasn't even noon.

He was willing to cut the man a break though. Having a coworker murdered was a gut punch.

"How long have you known Ms. Moyer?" Lance asked.

"Oh, well, almost five years now. She began working here right out of college if I recall. Worked her way up from clerk to assistant manager."

Knauer circled the desk, putting it between Lance and himself. The room wasn't particularly large, but it was a corner office with two large windows overlooking the resort's tennis court. It struck him that someone, probably Holly, had done their best to make the office feel welcoming. A brightly colored painting of Carling Lake hung on the wall opposite the desk and the standard-issue blinds had been spruced up with orange curtains. A bouquet of silk roses adorned the top of the file cabinet in the corner of the room and a plug-in spritzed strawberry scent into the air. A stack of mail sat on Holly's desk, a travel magazine on top.

When Lance arrived at the resort, he'd met Knauer in the manager's office, which had been nowhere near as spacious or nice as Holly's. Now, why would the resort manager allow the assistant manager to have a better office?

"Was Holly concerned about anyone? Maybe a guest who was particularly difficult or paid her unwanted attention." He pushed the magazine on top of the pile so he could read the return address on the envelope below.

Knauer frowned. Reaching across the desk, he slid the pile out of Lance's reach. "No. Absolutely not."

"That's a lot of mail. Has Holly been on vacation recently?"

"No, not at all. Holly is one of the resort's most dedicated employees. She rarely took a day off."

"Then why all the unopened mail?"

Knauer swallowed hard. "I... Holly and I didn't have the typical manager, assistant manager relationship. We divided responsibilities based on our strengths."

Lance quirked an eyebrow. "And Holly's strength wasn't responding to correspondence?"

"No."

Knauer's answer was weak. He suspected there was more to it. "I ask because we haven't yet determined why Holly was in Carling Lake. Would you have any idea about that?"

"Wha— How would I know?" A fine sheen of sweat had developed on Knauer's upper lip. "We were coworkers, but I don't know what she did in her free time."

"You seem nervous, Mr. Knauer. Is there a reason for that?"

"Well, of course I am. I've just found out my assistant manager was murdered. It's a distressing situation."

Maybe. But Lance didn't believe that was all there was to it. Instinct was telling him Knauer was hiding something. "Of course. And I won't keep you. I just have a few more questions." Before he asked his next question, a business card on Holly's desk caught his eye. "Does the resort work with Zane Goodman?"

A look of confusion swept across Knauer's face. Lance pointed to the card on Holly's desk.

"Oh, yes. We recently updated our website. Holly was the point person. She met with Mr. Goodman and supervised his work."

Lance jotted a note to speak to Zane Goodman. "Could Holly have been in Carling Lake to meet with Mr. Goodman?"

Knauer frowned. "I suppose it's possible, but I

don't see why. The website project was completed weeks ago."

But it gave a place to start figuring out why Holly had been in Carling Lake. Maybe a relationship had blossomed between her and Zane while they'd been working together.

"Maybe she mentioned dating someone in Carling Lake?"

"No way," Knauer snapped. "The suggestion is… It's ludicrous."

Lance studied the man, a suspicion growing. "Why would a young woman dating be a ludicrous suggestion, Mr. Knauer?"

Possibly realizing his reaction to the question had been over-the-top, Knauer stiffened. He smoothed his tie, visibly setting his expression to neutral. "I… It's not. I just meant Holly wasn't the kind of young woman that dated around."

"Was she dating you, Mr. Knauer?"

Knauer's cheeks mottled with color. "I can't… That you'd even suggest… I'm a married man… I…"

Lance held up a hand to stop the sputtering. "Mr. Knauer, I'm not trying to embarrass you or pass judgment here. I just need the truth so I can find the person who took Holly's life."

Knauer visibly deflated. "If my wife finds out…"

"I'll do my best to be discreet. I only care about finding a murderer."

Knauer dropped his gaze to the floor, guilt written across his face. "We were together once."

"You were having an affair."

Knauer's head snapped up. "Not an affair, no. Just, I don't know what it was, a couple of times we lost our heads."

Lance noted the change from "just once" to "a couple of times." "What else did you lose?"

Knauer's face paled. "What do you mean?"

"This office. The distribution of work between you and Holly?" He let the question hang out there unasked.

Knauer looked away. "We slept together and then Holly started pressing me for favors. Not really asking, you know, just like saying it would be nice if she didn't have to handle the mail correspondence. Or putting in for days off when she didn't have any more days banked." He slapped his forehead with the palm of his hand. "I was so stupid."

That explained the office. Holly was extorting Knauer.

"Mr. Knauer, did your wife know about your affair?"

The look of horror on the man's face could not have been faked. "No. No. And I don't want her to. It was a stupid mistake. You can't ruin my life over a mistake."

The way Lance saw it, it was Knauer who'd ruined his own life, if it was ruined at all. He had no sympathy for cheaters. There wasn't anything he could do about Knauer's fidelity. But if Knauer's wife knew about the affair, she had a motive to kill Holly. It wouldn't explain the card, but it wouldn't be the first time a killer had tried to throw law enforcement off track. He'd have to speak to Mrs. Knauer, and unless she was completely obtuse, she'd figure out her husband had strayed.

"Mr. Knauer, where were you between nine last night and six this morning?"

Knauer fell into the desk chair, his head in his hands. "I can't believe this."

"Mr. Knauer, please answer my question."

"Last night I was home with my wife and kids all night. I got home around six and I didn't leave for work until seven thirty this morning." He let his hands fall from his face. "Are we done?"

"For now," Lance said. At the door, he turned back. "I'll be in touch."

He left the resort and headed for the *Carling Lake Weekly* offices.

It wasn't until the doors of the elevator opened and he saw that Zane and Margaret Goodman were the only two people in the office that he realized he'd been looking forward to seeing Simone.

Zane sat with his back to the elevators, but his mother, Margaret, looked up as Lance strolled toward them.

"Sheriff Webb, how nice to see you." Margaret's smile was wide and bright. She was a woman who was always cheerful, but underneath the perennial smile, he detected a will of steel.

"Margaret, you are looking lovely today."

Margaret glowed. "How can I help you?"

"Actually, I'm here to talk to Zane." He turned to face the other man.

At the sound of his name, Zane finally looked away from his computer. "Me?"

"Yes. Do you have a minute now?"

Margaret picked up the mug on her desk. "I need a cup of coffee. I'll be in the kitchen if anyone needs me."

Zane watched his mother's retreating form, chewing his bottom lip. "What did you want to ask me about?"

"Your name came up in relation to an investigation. I don't know if you've heard but Holly Moyer's body has been found. We are treating the death as a homicide."

Sweat beaded on the man's forehead. "You want to ask me something? About a homicide? I don't know anything about any murder."

Lance placed a hand on Zane's shoulder. "Relax. It came up in my interviews of the employees at the Fairmont Inn & Resort that you did their web page for them."

"Yeah, I did," Zane said, leeriness in his tone.

"I just wondered if you knew Holly Moyer. Could you tell me anything about her?"

Zane relaxed a bit. "I met with her a few times. She was the point person on the project. Let's see, I met with her initially so she could tell me what the resort was looking for in updating its website. Most of our contact occurred over the phone though. I met her one other time to show her a mock-up and get suggestions for changes. And then I did a presentation at the resort once the site was ready to go live to show her and the manager how to use the administrator tools."

"Did you happen to see anything odd or suspicious when you were there? Holly arguing with anyone or any tension between her and another person?"

Zane shook his head. "No. Like I said, I wasn't around much."

"Were the two of you ever involved? Maybe go out on a date?"

"No. Never. I told you I only met with her a few times. Only about the work I was doing for the resort."

"Thanks," Lance said with more than a little frustration seeping through his tone.

Lance left the *Weekly*'s offices frustrated. So far he had little to go on. Nothing pointed conclusively, or even strongly, toward a suspect in Holly Moyer's murder.

And yet she had been murdered.

Could a twenty-years dormant serial killer really be back? And if so, why now?

He got into his sheriff's department vehicle, started the engine, and headed for the station.

Serial killer or no, someone had murdered Holly and he was going to do his damnedest to find out who.

Chapter Seven

Simone parked on the street in front of Lakeside Books and the small apartment above it that she rented. Sophie Hok, the building's owner and Simone's landlord, had already closed for the day as had most of the stores on the street. Once the height of the tourist season ended, most Carling Lake businesses happily went back to rolling up the sidewalks at six. There was only a smattering of people on the sidewalks downtown now, on an evening stroll, window-shopping or heading out for dinner.

Simone grabbed her messenger bag from the back seat of the 4Runner and reached for the door. Her phone beeped the receipt of an incoming text message. She pulled the phone from her bag.

BACK OFF IF YOU KNOW WHAT'S GOOD FOR YOU.

A chill rolled up her back. Suddenly she had the feeling she was being watched. She scanned the street through the windshield. A man on the corner wearing a ball cap pulled down low looked in her direction. Had he sent the text?

The man held her gaze for a moment longer, then turned away, walking in the opposite direction.

She tried to calm her racing heart. He was probably just a late-season tourist.

But someone had sent the text.

Brian Byers, possibly? He'd made it clear he didn't like that she was writing an article on his mother's murder. And the look on his face as she was leaving his aunt's house… Another chill shook her shoulders.

She got out of the car, her eyes darting over the street, unnaturally fearful that someone might jump out at her. But she saw no one suspicious as she rushed to open the door leading to her upper-level apartment. The man in the ball cap had vanished and she was alone on the street.

She climbed the stairs and reached her apartment without incident. There were two units above the bookshop, but the other apartment had been vacant since she'd moved in. Unlocking the door, she stepped into the front living room, its lights ablaze. The sound of the shower running and the indeterminate sounds of music came from the back of the apartment. For a moment she froze in place, but it was unlikely the texter had broken in to take a shower.

She shut and locked the door, chucking her bag and shoes and padding silently down the carpeted hallway to the bathroom.

The door was open, the original yellow flower-shaped sink and one-inch yellow-and-brown mosaic tiles a reminder of the apartment's desperate need for updating.

Lance stood behind the clear plastic shower liner in the garishly yellow bathtub, singing along to Drake's "Way 2 Sexy" playing on the iPhone balanced on the sink.

And Lance was, in fact, way too sexy for his own good. Or rather her own good. It was getting harder and harder to keep her feelings for the man at bay. His eyes were closed and turned upward at the showerhead, water flowing over hardened muscle and smooth brown skin. The clear shower curtain couldn't have paid off better.

She leaned against the door frame, watching the beautiful man in her shower. She smiled to herself, recalling how they'd met. She'd been on her first assignment for the *Weekly*, a write-up on an art show at the West Gallery. Lance had been there as a guest of the gallery's owner, his friend James West.

There'd been an instant and electric connection. She'd honestly had no intention of taking things any further than flirting that night, but then he'd offered her a ride home and insisted on walking her to her door. She'd turned back to face him and say goodnight after opening her door.

That was when she saw it in his eyes: lust. The same lust she'd been holding back all evening.

What should have been one crazy night had been going on for nearly three months now.

Lance had admonished her more than once about leaving a spare key under the fire extinguisher outside her front door, but she was glad he'd used it to let himself in. She hated to admit it, but the earlier text had shaken her. She was happy not to have to spend the night alone.

But that begged the question of whether she should tell Lance about the text. It was a threat for sure, but she'd received worse. And Lance was bound to over-react. He'd already caught her going to great lengths for a story. She couldn't imagine what he'd do if he knew about this text and her connection to the Card Killer's last victim. For now, it seemed the best course of action was to add the text to the growing list of secrets she was keeping from the sheriff.

Lance turned off the shower and pulled back the liner, reaching for the towel hanging just outside the shower.

His handsome face spread into a smile when he noticed her in the doorway.

"Peeping is illegal, you know."

She grinned. "Arrest me."

His light brown eyes darkened with desire as he wrapped the towel around his waist, and she fought the urge to pout.

Crossing the small bathroom in two strides, he planted a kiss on her lips that burned with promise.

His phone buzzed and he broke off their kiss, took a quick step back and grabbed it.

His lips quirked down in a small frown as he typed out a quick message.

"Work?" She kept her tone casual, although the thought of him leaving brought on an instant surge of disappointment. They'd fallen into a comfortable, if surreptitious, pattern of dinner at her place two or three times a week and she'd begun to look forward to those nights more than she wanted to admit.

"No." He tapped the screen a few more times before shifting his attention back to her. "I'm off duty until morning."

He palmed the phone and dropped another kiss on her lips before crossing the narrow hall between the primary bedroom and the bathroom.

"I have leftover lasagna and garlic bread in the fridge. Could you warm it up while I change?" She headed for the shower.

She stripped and hopped into the shower, still thinking about how protective he was of his phone, which wasn't necessarily unusual for a cop, but it still spiked her curiosity. She knew he wasn't married; she'd done her homework on the sheriff. But that didn't mean there wasn't another woman or other women for that matter.

They'd never broached the subject of exclusivity, and why should they? Whatever they had couldn't last.

She got out of the shower and padded to the bedroom. She could hear Lance moving around in the kitchen as she pulled on leggings and a T-shirt and maneuvered her chin-length bob into a French braid.

The smell of cheese and marinara sauce hit her as she made her way to the kitchen.

He'd changed into a clean T-shirt and a pair of

black shorts and was sliding the garlic bread out of the oven as she entered.

"Perfect timing. I'm starving." He cut slices of bread and added them to the plates of lasagna he'd already set out.

Simone grabbed two glasses from a cabinet and filled each with red wine from the bottle Lance had already opened, then carried them to the table.

Simone set the glasses on the trunk-slash-coffee table next to their plates and sat on the couch beside Lance.

For the first several minutes, they ate in silence, Simone unaware of just how hungry she'd been until the spicy sausage in the lasagna permeated her taste buds.

"How was the rest of your day?"

Lance eyed her over the rim of his wineglass. "You know you have to contact the sheriff's office press liaison for information on a case."

Simone raised her hands. "I only asked about your day." She reached for her wineglass. "But since you brought it up...did you identify the victim?"

"What part of press liaison didn't you understand?" He speared a corner of lasagna with his fork.

"If the press liaison can release the name, surely the sheriff can too. You'd save me a phone call in the morning."

He smiled wryly and sighed. "Holly Moyer, but you can't use it until tomorrow morning. We've already contacted the family. The press release will go out tomorrow morning."

"Got it." She'd make sure her article was online the minute the press release went out. She'd still beat Eugene and every other reporter to the story. "Do you have a confirmed cause of death yet?" The pictures she'd taken made it clear that Holly had suffered a significant amount of trauma to her neck, but she'd need confirmation from the sheriff's department or the ME on the official cause of death.

Lance laid his fork on his empty plate and used a napkin to wipe his mouth before looking her in the eye. "Simone, I think you should tread carefully. This case, it may not be what it seems."

Her reporter's antenna went up. "What do you mean?" Was he about to admit Holly Moyer's murder was connected to the Card Killer cases?

He hesitated. "I mean someone killed Holly Moyer. There's a dangerous person out there and I don't want you to get hurt."

She pushed her plate away. "I have to do my job just like you do."

"My job is supposed to be dangerous. Yours isn't."

"Tell that to the scores of reporters who have put their lives on the line to report a story." Not to mention the ones who'd lost their lives. She crossed her arms over her chest. "I'm going to do my job the best way I know how, so just let it go, okay?"

For a moment he looked like he was going to argue with her, but then his eyes swept over hers and he let out a heavy sigh.

"I don't want to fight."

He stood, reaching for her as he did. She let him pull her up and then into his chest.

She could see genuine concern and fear for her safety.

Her pique dimmed.

She placed a hand lightly on his biceps and felt the muscle tense. "I don't want to fight either."

He stepped closer until there was no more than a breath between them.

She feathered a light kiss against his lips.

"You take too many risks, break too many rules—eventually that catches up to you, Simone."

"Maybe," she said, kissing him again, but this time there was nothing light about it. "But not tonight."

Chapter Eight

Buoyed by an invigorating round of early-morning sex, Lance made his way home to change before heading into the station. The case was proving to be a web of dead ends and false starts. He'd gone to the Knauer residence after leaving the Fairmont the day before and spoken to Libby Knauer. He'd had to ask the woman if she knew about the affair her husband had had with Holly. The stunned look on her face had been enough to convince him she was telling the truth when she'd said she didn't. Which meant she hadn't had a motive to kill Holly that he could see. She'd also confirmed Fred's alibi, which left Lance grasping for another suspect.

In his office, he found the message indicator on his phone glowing an ominous red. A message from Barber promising preliminary results from Holly Moyer's autopsy by that afternoon awaited him along with a message from former sheriff Matt Reeser. He'd left a message for his former boss and mentor the previous afternoon asking to meet and go over his notes and reports on the Card Killer case. Reeser's message stated that he was available all day and that Lance should stop by whenever it was convenient for him.

Since time was of the essence in a murder investigation, he got on the road right away. Forty-five minutes later he turned into the former Carling Lake sheriff's unpaved driveway.

Reeser lived in a large farmhouse set back off the road and surrounded by nothing but open fields as far as the eye could see. Fresh white paint trimmed the windows accented by vibrant blue shutters. Large planters with a colorful array of flowers sat on either side of the front door. A swing hung from the roof of the porch, swaying lightly in the early fall breeze. The former sheriff obviously put time and effort into the upkeep of the residence.

Lance parked behind a dusty blue pickup truck and made his way along a gray stone pathway to the front door of the house.

He pressed the doorbell and waited.

The door swung open. It had been years since he'd taken over the job of sheriff from Matt Reeser, but the former sheriff hadn't changed much. In his late sixties now, Reeser was almost a foot shorter than Lance. He wore a faded plaid shirt and weathered jeans. Rimless spectacles sat on the end of his fleshy nose and the once straggling strands of hair covering his head had apparently given up the ghost, leaving the former sheriff completely bald.

Reeser smiled a toothy grin. "Sheriff Webb. Good to see you."

"It's still something to hear you call me Sheriff," Lance said, shaking the older man's hand.

"That's who you are now and a damn good sheriff from what I've heard."

"If I am, it's because you trained me well."

"Oh, now." Reeser waved away the compliment and led Lance into an open-concept living-dining-kitchen space. "Come on in. Have a seat." He pointed to a dining table that was already set with two place settings and food. "I know it's a drive out here and back, so I prepared a little something in case you were hungry. Mango Toast with Hazelnut-Pepita Butter." The former sheriff settled into a chair at the head of the table.

"Look at you, Chef Ramsey." Lance slid into the chair to Reeser's left.

"Not much to do out here except take care of the house and watch too much television. I've taken a liking to the cooking shows, especially that young woman Rachael Ray. Her recipes aren't half bad."

Lance popped a piece of toast in his mouth and chewed. "If this is an example of her work, I have to agree."

Reeser pushed one of the bottled waters on the table and a glass toward Lance. "I doubt you've come all this way to talk about recipes. What can I do for you?"

He'd given only the barest of details in his message to Reeser, but if the former sheriff watched as much television as he said he did, he'd undoubtedly heard about the body they'd found the day before.

"I'm investigating a murder. You've heard about the body found in Watercress yesterday?"

Reeser nodded. "Saw it on the news last night."

"I have reason to believe there might be a connection between my current murder and three murders that occurred in Carling Lake twenty years ago."

Reeser jerked in surprise. "What reason?"

Lance pulled the evidence bag with the card from the file folder he'd carried in from his car. "This was found with the body of Holly Moyer yesterday. Do you recognize it?"

Reeser reached for the bag and studied the card inside for a long moment. "I don't recognize this particular card, but I can say that it is similar to the ones we found with the bodies twenty years ago." Reeser's eyes rose to meet Lance's. "Very similar."

"That's what I thought too when I looked at it next to the evidence in the prior cases. The forensics reports on the older cards said they appeared to be homemade on someone's printer."

Reeser massaged his chin. "Yes. If I remember correctly, the cards were a dead end. The paper was thicker than normal but could be bought at any office supply store. It had obviously been cut down to size, but that information was of no help. The skull is a skull." Reeser held his hands up in a helpless gesture. "We tracked down a few artists to see if they'd designed it. That went nowhere. I suspected the killer designed the cards himself. It would have been easy enough to do with all the different graphic design programs out there now."

Reeser handed the card back to Lance.

"I've read the file, but I'd like to hear your take on it. Your impressions, theories."

Reeser sighed. "Twenty years is a long time, Webb."

"Anything you can remember," Lance said, opening his notebook, ready to take notes.

"If I had to rely on my memory, you'd be out of luck. Lucky for you, I kept a copy of my notes. Reviewed 'em before you arrived." Reeser pulled a folder from the seat of the chair on the other side of the table.

The sheriff's department's policy said that all notes should be kept in the official file in the office, but it wasn't unusual for investigators to make notes as things came to them or to even make a copy of their notes to keep at home. It wasn't a sanctioned practice, but it was a widespread one.

"There were no fingerprints or any other evidence at any of the crime scenes that pointed to a suspect," Lance said, getting the ball rolling.

"Nothing. And believe me, we looked. Hard. It was like this killer was a ghost. No fingerprints or other forensics, which, as you know, was not easy to do even twenty years ago. Nobody saw anything. Nobody heard anything. These women were just going about their lives and then they were gone." Reeser shook his head, his expression a mixture of sadness and anger that Lance could relate to. "Is the card the only reason you think your recent murder is connected to the prior murders?"

"Holly Moyer appears to have been strangled by something thin. Possibly a wire," Lance answered with a pointed look. "The ME will hopefully have something more definitive for me later today, but…"

"But with the twentieth anniversary of the earlier murders on the horizon and the similarities…" Reeser nodded his understanding.

"It's possible, maybe not probable but possible, the killer has returned to town."

Reeser's eyebrow arched. "If he ever left."

"Why do you say that? Based on the case notes, the general consensus was that the killer must have left town—maybe voluntarily moving along so he didn't get caught—landed himself in jail or died."

Reeser took a long pull of his root beer, then leaned back in his chair. "I know that's what the notes say. That's what the state profiler concluded when we ran out of leads to pursue after the last victim was found."

"Nancy Oliver."

"Yes." Reeser nodded. "I was a young sheriff. I'd barely had the position for two years when the first murder occurred. I deferred to the more experienced law enforcement officials, but I've always wondered."

Lance leaned forward, his interest piqued. Reeser had always had admirable instincts born of experience and a natural talent for sniffing out when suspects were holding back. It was one of the things Lance had admired most about the sheriff when he'd worked under him. If Reeser felt like something was wrong or overlooked in the conclusions drawn in the prior case, that was something Lance wanted to look into.

"What do you wonder?"

"How the killer got his victims." Reeser ran his index finger around the rim of his root beer can as he spoke. "These women weren't careless. Yes, Carling Lake is a safe community, but these weren't women who would just get into a car with a stranger or be easily lured to some out-of-the-way place. And yet each one was killed at a place where you wouldn't expect to find them in the middle of the night."

Lance saw where Reeser was headed. "So you think the killer was someone they knew and trusted enough to meet at night."

Reeser nodded. "Which points heavily in the direction of someone who lived in the community."

It made sense. And it also fit with his current murder. Holly worked at the Fairmont, which employed quite a few Carling Lake residents. It was possible someone she knew, someone she trusted who lived in Carling Lake, lured her to town and killed her. But who? And why?

"The profiler's working theory on the killer's motive seemed to be that he was driven by a need to punish women he felt weren't living pious or righteous enough lives. That is how he explained the words written on the cards. Did you agree with that theory?"

Reeser shrugged. "It was the best we had to go on."

Not a ringing endorsement of the profiler's skills.

"The press loved it. They are the ones who dubbed the guy the Card Killer," Reeser added with more than a hint of disgust ringing in his voice.

"All the women were so different, but someone knew enough about each of them to leave these cards with perceived offenses if we assume the theory is correct."

"We tore through the victims' lives. Every one of them had people in their lives who could have killed them, but we couldn't find a common person who'd want all three of them dead."

"The report said you looked into Juanita Byers's husband, but he had an alibi. What about the other two victims?"

"Byers's husband looked good on paper, but he was in the county jail at the time and didn't have a motive to kill the other women that we could find. He didn't have a motive to kill Juanita. By all accounts, he was a cheater with a gambling addiction and a petty criminal, but everyone we talked to said he did love his wife."

"Your notes said she'd been let go from her job for stealing. And her husband was in jail for passing bad checks. That could explain why the killer left the Greed card with Juanita's body."

"Could." Reeser looked thoughtful. "Although I never bought that Juanita was a thief. I didn't know her well, but she was a fine woman. As straight an arrow as there ever was."

"And the other victims?" Lance said, writing.

"Deborah Indigo had been rumored to be having an affair, but if she was, I could never confirm it."

"And Nancy?"

Reeser sighed heavily. "Nancy was a troubled young woman. Tough home life. But she was a good soul and smart as a whip. She drank too much, like a lot of young people around these parts. I believe she would have gotten herself together if she hadn't been killed so young."

Lance looked up from his notes. "And you couldn't find a single person connecting these women."

Reeser shook his head. "Not a one."

"Which means if the killer was a Carling Lake resident, it's someone who knew these women but likely wasn't very close to them."

"That's what I think, which makes everyone in town a suspect. Almost everyone knows everyone at least by sight. And the way the gossip mill churns in town…"

Reeser left the rest of the thought unsaid. Carling Lake was like any other town when it came to gossip, yet if Reeser's theory was correct, someone had managed to keep a very big secret for two decades.

"I wish I could have helped you more."

Lance scooped the card back into the case folder and gave the former sheriff a tight smile. "Just talking the prior cases through with you has helped."

Lance followed Reeser to the door.

Reeser stopped at the front door without opening it. "Look, I don't want to give unsolicited advice because I wouldn't have taken kindly to it when I was sheriff, but I'm going to do it anyway. The Card Killer set this town on tinders twenty years ago. People were terrified and the political powers that be came down on me something fierce to find the killer. Ackerman Hanes was mayor then. He'd passed away before you joined the department, but his daughter, Melinda, the current mayor, is just as much a political climber and possibly even more ruthless."

"Yeah, I got a visit from Madam Mayor yesterday all but demanding I find the killer fast and not so much as think the words *card* or *killer*."

The worry lines on Reeser's forehead deepened. "Just watch your back. I'm here to help however I can."

"I appreciate it."

Lance's phone beeped an incoming text as he reached for the door to the SUV. He got into the car but read the text before turning on the engine. He immediately wished he hadn't.

The text was from Deputy Bridges, showing a video of a breaking news segment from Channel WRCW. Eugene Ryan stood in front of the sheriff's department, but Lance didn't need to listen to the reporter's words to know that the you-know-what had hit the fan. The chyron at the bottom of the screen said it all.

Authorities suspect the Card Killer has returned.

Chapter Nine

Simone had barely stepped into the *Weekly* when Aaron's voice boomed from his office.

"Simone. Get in here!"

Zane looked at her from behind the glass wall of the conference room where he worked with a pitying expression.

"What's wrong?"

From behind his desk, Aaron pointed at the television in the corner of the office.

Simone followed his finger and saw Eugene's face on the screen. He was standing in front of the sheriff's department with the words *Authorities suspect Card Killer in recent homicide* across the bottom of the screen.

Simone's stomach fell.

"The sheriff's department has issued no official comment to our inquiry, but sources tell us that a possible connection has been made between the murder of Holly Moyer, the young woman whose body was found near the Watercress neighborhood just yesterday, and the Card Killer, who stalked the town of Carling Lake nearly twenty years ago to the day."

Aaron paused the television. "Why didn't you know about this?"

"I—"

"I hired you because I thought you were a shark," Aaron cut her off. "So we could compete with the local stations with our online content and possibly increase circulation. So how come the networks have a scoop that we seem to know nothing about?"

"I'm sorry. I knew there was a possibility of a connection, but—"

"Then why didn't I know?" Aaron's voice was thunderous. "Maybe keeping pertinent information about a story from your editor is something that was encouraged in the big city, but I've got news for you— that's not how I operate."

"I know and I shouldn't have. I just wanted to run down the lead a bit more before I brought it to you."

Aaron's usually fair skin flamed red. "Have you run it down enough? Because Eugene Ryan has run it down enough. He doesn't even live in Carling Lake and he's standing in front of our sheriff's department scooping us."

"I'm sorry—"

"I don't want to hear it. Since you apparently need a refresher on how a newsroom works, here it goes. You go out and chase the stories, then you bring back all the information you've found and I decide what is important enough to be printed. Got it?"

Simone gritted her teeth. She was wrong for having kept the possible connection to the Card Killer from Aaron, but she didn't appreciate the condescension.

"Look, Aaron, I know I messed up."

"You got that right," he huffed. "If this is what you do on what could be the biggest story in Carling Lake in the last twenty years, I'm not sure I made the right decision in hiring you."

She felt sick. Aaron was right. She'd let her connection to this case cloud her professional judgment. And now she could be on the precipice of losing her job for it.

"I have something the news station doesn't have." She pulled her phone from her messenger bag and called up the crime scene photos that showed the playing card next to Holly Moyer's body.

He studied the photos for more than a minute, a range of emotions traveling over his face as he did. Shock. Horror. And then anger again when he realized she had to have taken the photos a day earlier and kept them from him. Simone wasn't sure that the next words out of his mouth wouldn't be "you're fired" by the time he looked up from the photos.

"We are not finished discussing this. Right now I want you to write something up to post with these photos online and I want it within the hour. Oh, and don't forget you're covering the political event for Nikki King at West Gallery tonight."

She hadn't forgotten, but she had planned to beg out of the event, maybe suggest it would be a good work-slash-date-night thing for Aaron to take Margaret to. But that no longer seemed like a wise course of action given the circumstances.

"I haven't forgotten. I'll be there," she clipped out.

She turned and strode from Aaron's office engulfed in a mixture of anger at the tone he'd used and embarrassment for having messed up so badly.

She could feel Zane's eyes on her as she left the *Weekly*'s offices. She'd messed up, but she could fix it. Or at least beat Eugene and WRCW to the next big break in the story.

The WRCW news van was still parked at the curb in front of the sheriff's department when Simone arrived, but Eugene was nowhere in sight. She took that as a positive sign and entered the station. The waiting area was crowded with residents and the station's phones seemed to be ringing incessantly.

Simone fought her way to the front of the reception desk.

"Yes, I understand, but the sheriff is not available. Would you like to leave a message?"

The voice on the other end of the line was loud enough to be heard and Simone wasn't shocked when the clerk didn't write down the less than decorous message.

The clerk picked up the next call without so much as looking at the group waiting in front of her desk. "Sheriff's Department. Hold, please. Sheriff's Department. Hold, please. Sheriff's Department. Hold, please." The clerk answered calls in rapid succession.

She had less than an hour to get her story to Aaron. The crowd of people around the desk blocked the clerk's view of the door leading to Lance's office. She knew from experience the door wasn't usually locked. She slipped behind the group and over to the door. The handle turned easily in her hand.

The deputies were just as busy answering phone calls as the clerk out front. Neither of the two who were currently at their desks even looked up as she passed by on her way to Lance's office.

She glanced into a conference room as she passed and froze.

Several boxes had been stacked in a corner and several files were spread out on the long conference table in the center of the room. But that was not what had stopped her in her tracks.

Photos of Deborah Indigo, Juanita Byers, Nancy Oliver and Holly Moyer hung on a bulletin board on the far wall of the room. Two photos of each woman. One of each woman alive and a second showing the cruel brutality of their deaths.

Her gaze locked on Nancy's photos. She walked into the conference room and stopped in front of the board.

The image of Nancy clawing at her neck, terror shining in her eyes, had haunted her for twenty years. It had kept her awake countless nights and run on a loop through her nightmares.

Her gaze moved to Holly's photograph. And now the same killer may have taken another life.

If only she had said something. If she'd insisted that her mother listen and take her seriously. Or gone to the sheriff on her own.

But she hadn't and Holly may have paid the price for her cowardice.

A tear slid over her cheek. "I should have said something. I'm so sorry."

"Simone."

She spun around.

Lance stood behind her. His eyes raked over her face.

"You should have said something about what?"

"WHAT SHOULD YOU have said, Simone?"

"I... Nothing. I was just talking to myself," she said, flustered and surprised to feel wetness on her face.

"I heard. It sounded like you think you know something pertinent to my case."

She wiped the tears from her cheeks. "No. Not at all. It's just seeing them all up there like that."

He didn't believe her for a moment. This case had gotten to her. It was more than just a story to her. What he couldn't figure out was what she wouldn't say. He didn't like that she was keeping secrets from him.

"You shouldn't be in here." His tone was icy.

She jerked and her back stiffened. "I'm sorry. I was just coming to get a quote from you for the paper."

"No comment." He gestured to the door. Although she hadn't broken the news of a possible connection between the current and past murders, he was in no mood to deal with the press, not even Simone, right now.

She didn't move. "You don't even know the story I'm asking for a quote for."

He quirked an eyebrow. "I can hazard a guess. You want me to confirm that this office is investigating a possible connection between Holly Moyer's murder and the Card Killer murders. My answer is no comment."

She cocked her head. "I don't need you to confirm a possible connection. I know for a fact there's a possible connection." She pulled her phone from her bag and called up a photo. "The *Weekly* is going to run this photo from Holly Moyer's crime scene."

He was looking at a picture of the card he'd shown Reeser just a little while earlier, taken with a long lens from the looks of it. The damn tree house. He should have anticipated she'd taken pictures.

"We won't have to state that there's a connection. Everyone will be able to figure that out for themselves."

He looked up from the picture. "You can't publish this. The town will erupt."

"Have you taken a look at your lobby? The town is already erupting." She took her phone from his hands.

"Simone."

She held up her hand. "It's not up to me. Aaron has seen the photo. The picture goes up in—" she looked at the time on the phone "—twenty-eight minutes whether you make a statement or not."

"No comment," he gritted out.

Simone sighed heavily. "I have to do my job."

"And if you publish that, you'll be making my job harder."

She looked at him with sad eyes. "I'm afraid your

job is about to get very difficult no matter what I do or don't do. The residents are going to come after you with pitchforks either way."

He blew out a deep breath. "You can print that we found a card similar to the type found with three other unsolved homicides. The sheriff's office is investigating whether there is a connection. We encourage Carling Lake residents to remain calm but vigilant, and ask that anyone with information please contact the sheriff's office."

She squeezed his biceps. "Thank you."

He lowered his head until his forehead touched hers. "I'm worried about you. For you. I know there's something you're not telling me."

"Lance—"

"No, just listen. I'm not asking you to tell me what it is. At least not yet. But I want you to know that you can tell me. You can trust me."

He was close enough to hear her breath catch. Her eyes held his and he saw the moment she decided to let him in.

His phone rang, ruining the moment.

Simone stepped back.

He swore silently before pulling the phone from his back pocket. "I'm sorry. I have to take this."

"It's fine. I should go. I have to get my article to Aaron." She slid past him toward the door.

His finger hovered over the button to connect the call. "Simone?"

She turned.

There was so much he wanted to say. That he had a

bad feeling about this case. That he was scared she'd attract the attention of the killer. That he was falling in love with her.

But every one of those statements opened a door they didn't have the time to walk through right now.

"Be careful."

Chapter Ten

Figuring Aaron hadn't had a sufficient amount of time to cool off, Simone found an empty bench in the commons across from the sheriff's department and pulled her laptop from her messenger bag. One thing ten years in the business had given her was the ability to get a story out from anywhere and under almost any conditions. She tapped out a nine-hundred-word article revealing that a skull playing card much like the one found with the Card Killer's victims had been found with Holly Moyer, including the official statement Lance had given her. Two minutes before Aaron's stated deadline, she emailed the article and the photo to him, then headed for her car.

Lance said he was worried about her. Well, she was worried about herself. She'd jeopardized her career by not telling Aaron about the playing card found next to Holly's body. Hell, she was jeopardizing her career by sneaking around with the town sheriff. Not to mention putting whatever they might be building in jeopardy, while keeping her connection to Nancy Oliver from him.

She should come clean. Tell Aaron and Lance the whole truth and let the chips fall where they may. Aaron would almost certainly take her off the story for having a conflict of interest. And Lance?

Would he end whatever it was they were doing when he found out she'd been keeping pertinent information from him about a case?

Which was why she couldn't tell either of them the truth yet. She owed it to Nancy to do whatever she could to reinvigorate the Card Killer investigation and finally identify the killer. And if her silence was the reason that the killer had escaped justice long enough to kill Holly Moyer, then she owed it to Holly too. The possible damage to her career and her fledgling relationship with Lance weren't nearly as important.

She needed to know more about Holly. Who was she? How had she had the misfortune to cross paths with a killer? Did she have any connection to the women killed twenty years ago? Right now the only thing Simone knew for sure was that Holly had worked at the Fairmont, so that was where she'd start.

The Fairmont Inn & Resort was situated about halfway between Stunnersville and Carling Lake. The thirty-two-acre property boasted hiking and horse-back riding trails, indoor and outdoor pools, a luxury spa and two five-star restaurants among many other amenities. Although she hadn't lived in the area at the time, Simone knew its construction and grand opening a little more than six years ago had split the residents of Carling Lake. Some feared the new resort would lure away tourists who'd otherwise stay and spend money in Carling Lake. Others thought the resort would invigorate the economy, bringing in more visitors who'd be more than willing to make the thirty-minute drive to Carling Lake. So far it seemed like the latter group was right. The resort had not only seemed to increase tourism but had also provided a host of new employment opportunities for area residents. Now the big bone of contention at town council meetings was the increase in property values that the resort and the subsequent surrounding real estate boom had wrought.

Be careful what you wish for. The old admonition rolled through her head as she turned onto the resort property and navigated the 4Runner into a parking space.

She'd been to the resort on a couple of occasions covering various events. It was a place where a reporter asking questions would stand out like a commoner at the Queen's garden party. Not to mention that she doubted any of Holly's coworkers would dare answer her questions where they might be seen or overheard by management.

No, she'd need to take a more inconspicuous approach.

She got out of the car and, instead of heading for the resort's entrance, followed the paved pathway around the side of the building. Ocean-blue water rippled in the Olympic-sized outdoor pool. In the distance, a red-brick path led to tennis courts. Her eyes scanned over the scantily clad women sunning themselves poolside. She finally found what she was looking for. A gated area tucked behind some shrubs; a sign on the gate announced it as an employees-only section. She headed that way, slipping through the gate and into another world altogether. A concrete path led to a large back door with a second employees-only sign. Farther away along the path was a parking lot with cars not nearly as flashy as those in the lot at the front of the resort. The employee lot. She was in the right place.

She tried the door and unsurprisingly found it locked.

She made herself as comfortable as she could leaning against a nearby tree and waited. She gave thanks it was a warm sunny day when after forty-five minutes she still hadn't seen a single soul go in or out of the door. Finally, after more than an hour of waiting, the door opened.

A woman in a standard black skirt and white button-down shirt strode from the resort. She started for the concrete path leading to the employee parking lot and Simone hurried to catch up with her.

"Excuse me. Miss?"

The woman turned around, a polite if somewhat strained smile already fixed on her face. "Certainly. What can I do for you, ma'am?"

"My name is Simone Jarrett. I'm with the *Carling Lake Weekly.*"

The smile on the other woman's face fell. "I'm not supposed to talk to you." She began walking again.

"Please. I just have a few questions."

"A few questions could get me fired. Look, I just had to work an hour over my shift because the other front desk clerk had car trouble and came in late. I just want to go home and go to sleep, okay?"

"I don't have to use your name." Simone hurried to keep up with the woman. She was at least a couple of inches taller, but the other woman was motivated to get away.

But not as motivated as Simone was to talk to her. "You can be on deep background."

The woman's brows drew together. "What does that mean?"

"It means I won't use your name or indicate where I got any information you give me in any way."

"I'm not going to give you my name."

"I have to have your name. Just for me and my editor," Simone added quickly. "Those are the rules, but I promise no one else will know we spoke."

The woman hesitated for so long that Simone was sure she'd refuse to answer. Finally, she said, "Lindly Fowler."

She pulled out her notebook and wrote the name.

"Great. Thank you, Lindly. Now, I just want to know a little more about who Holly was. What she liked. What she didn't like. Who her friends were."

Lindly snorted and kept walking. "That's easy. She liked nothing. She found fault with everything. She had no friends."

The statement took Simone aback. She pictured the smiling young woman with blue eyes from the photo on Lance's bulletin board. The image didn't fit with the person the woman in front of her was describing.

"What do you mean?"

Lindly stopped walking again and turned to face Simone. "Holly was a b...witch. She treated everyone here like they were beneath her because she was management. Barking orders. Putting us down. Writing us up for any small mistake or violation of resort policy. She made the entire staff's lives a nightmare."

Holly's attitude toward her coworkers might explain the Pride card that was left with her body. But there was one thing that didn't make sense. "So why would the resort keep her on, then?"

Lindly smirked. "That's a great question. There are a bunch of theories, but the one that gets the most votes is that she was schtupping the manager, Fred Knauer."

Always a tried-and-true rumor about women in power. But just because it was crass didn't mean it wasn't true.

"Is Fred married?"

Lindly laughed. "Of course he is. Aren't they all?"

So someone who could have possibly had a motive for wanting to kill Holly, assuming their affair had gone badly. Which was a big assumption at the moment.

"Is there anyone who might have wanted to hurt Holly?"

"Haven't you been listening?" Lindly shot back. "Like, the entire staff. But I doubt anyone would actually kill her. I mean, your reporter friends are saying it was the Card Killer, like, come back from the dead or something."

"Right." That was the problem with floating possible theories. The Card Killer angle got eyes on the story, which meant revenue for newspapers and stations. But once the public latched on to a theory of the crime, they often overlooked other, sometimes more reasonable and likely, possibilities. "What about friends? Was there anyone Holly got along with? Someone who doesn't work at the resort maybe."

"Umm… I wouldn't know about that." The woman looked thoughtful. "I guess the one person who I'd say Holly got along with best is Arianna."

"Arianna?" Simone wrote the name and waited.

"Arianna Arjan. She's one of the concierges. She also wants Holly's job, which was why she was willing to be such a brownnoser. Kissing up to Holly even though we all knew she hated the woman as much as we did."

"Do you think that Arianna will get Holly's job now?"

Lindly shrugged. "Maybe. Things are more than a little off-kilter here right now. I mean we're all kind of spooked that someone we worked with was murdered, you know."

"Of course."

Lindly's eyes moved to the path they'd just come from. "Look, I have to go, alright? I've told you everything I know."

Simone doubted that was true, but she also knew she'd probably gotten everything she was going to get out of Lindly at the moment.

"Thank you."

"Don't forget. Deep background or whatever. We never spoke."

"We never spoke."

Simone watched the woman walk away before turning back the way she'd come. She went inside the Fairmont and asked to speak to Fred Knauer but was told he was unavailable. From the tone of Knauer's assistant's voice, it was clear Fred was going to be unavailable as long as Simone wanted to talk to him. She'd have to hunt him down another way.

She contemplated waiting for another employee to come out of the back door, but the desire to find out more about Arianna Arjan won out. She could always come back another day and stake out the employee entrance again.

Lindly had given her a possible lead. Maybe Arianna knew someone who might have had it out for Holly. Even if she didn't, she might know why Holly had been in Carling Lake two nights ago or if Holly had a connection to the Card Killer's earlier victims. Either way, she needed to talk to Arianna Arjan.

Lance signed in at the medical examiner's office and headed through the labyrinth of hallways to the basement-level morgue. The elevator doors opened to a brightly lit hallway undoubtedly designed to take one's mind off the sometimes disturbing but necessary work that was done there in the rooms beyond. No matter how bright the fluorescent lights, there was no masking the mixture of formaldehyde and decay that swirled through the hall.

Having learned early in his career that autopsies can be a messy business, he slid a blue hospital gown over his uniform before stepping into the room.

Barber was hunched over the body of an elderly man, speaking his findings into the microphone hanging from the ceiling.

Lance waited on the opposite side of the table for him to finish his thought.

"You suspect foul play?" Lance asked, nodding toward the body between him and Barber.

"Possibly," Barber answered from behind a face shield. "His son called for paramedics, saying he'd taken a fall down the stairs. Doctors at the hospital didn't buy the son's story and called the cops, who flagged it as a suspicious death. There is some bruising that I don't think can be explained by a fall, but I haven't completed my examination."

"Stunnersville PD?"

"Murrieta."

Barber was the district county medical examiner and as such served a number of the incorporated towns in the county. Lucky for Lance, the medical examiner's regional office was located just outside Carling Lake town limits, which made it easy for him to pop in when necessary.

"Your victim is over here." Barber turned, walking past an empty exam table before stopping at the third table in the room. He shed the disposable gloves he'd been wearing and donned a new pair, passing a pair to Lance as well.

"You noticed the bruises around her neck at the scene. She was strangled with some type of ligature."

Lance leaned forward so he could get a look at the bruises Barber pointed to. "Any idea what was used?"

"Something thin from the looks of it. Not a cloth, I'd say, but it's hard to tell. It left no discernible pattern, so—" Barber shrugged "—your guess is as good as mine."

"Could it have been a thin piece of wire?"

Barber's eyebrows arched up. "Still looking for a connection to the prior murders, huh?"

"Just doing my due diligence. I haven't ruled it out yet."

"A wire could have been used. Something smooth that didn't leave fibers behind. I took the liberty of pulling the autopsy records for the three women suspected of having been killed by the Card Killer and compared their autopsy results to Ms. Moyer's."

Lance smiled wryly at the doctor. "Now look who's looking for connection."

Barber chuckled. "The wounds are similar, but I can't say definitively that they were made by the same instrument. I can say the bruises are approximately the same width."

"Got anything on the toxicology screen?"

"Nothing on the screen. You know it will be a few weeks before the full toxicology results come back, but Ms. Moyer appears to have been a perfectly healthy young woman. Although there is one thing of note." Barber paused dramatically.

"Don't keep me in suspense, Doc."

"Ms. Moyer was pregnant. About six weeks along."

He was silent for a long moment. "Neither her parents nor her friend mentioned that she was pregnant."

"They may not have known. *She* may not have known. She was very early in the pregnancy." Barber looked at the body with sadness in his eyes.

Lance was skeptical. "At almost two months along? Seems unlikely though, right?"

He thought back on when he and his ex-wife, Jen, had been trying to start a family. Jen had been diligent about taking her temperature multiple times a day and keeping a calendar of her cycle. They'd spent a fortune on ovulation tests and take-home pregnancy tests and eventually more intrusive medical tests to no avail.

Barber shook his head. "If she'd never been pregnant before, she could have overlooked or dismissed the signs. She may not have missed her cycle yet."

He'd have to take Barber's word for it. "But if Holly did know she was pregnant, there might be a guy out there who was going to be a father and was not too thrilled about it."

"That's your area of expertise. I'm only here to give you the facts and it's a fact that Holly Moyer was pregnant at the time of her murder."

Chapter Eleven

Simone's wardrobe purposefully leaned toward comfort over style. Jeans and an assortment of sweaters, blouses and T-shirts, and a couple of pieces of nice but not expensive jewelry, comprised the bulk of it. She eyed the black dress in her closet, wondering whether it was the better choice for tonight. It would certainly be a more demure choice than the red A-line dress with a pleated skirt that she currently wore. It had been an impulse buy on a trip to Chicago not long before she'd accepted the job with the *Weekly*. The dress had called to her, and she couldn't bring herself to leave the store without it. Not that she'd had anyplace to wear it. At least, not until now.

James and Erika West were hosting a fundraiser and question and answer session for Carling Lake mayoral candidate Nikki King. Technically, Simone would be working, covering the fundraiser for the *Weekly*. But the event was being held at the swanky West Gallery, so she couldn't wear her usual jeans and top.

And Lance might be there and she wanted to look nice for him.

Which wasn't a crime. He usually saw her dressed down. Or in nothing at all. Since they were keeping their relationship quiet, they hadn't done the traditional going out to dinner date. This would be the first time he'd see her dolled up.

She took one more look at herself in the full-length mirror on the back of her bedroom door and added small gold hoop earrings to complete the outfit. She pinned her shoulder-length bob into an easy updo and swiped on a bit of makeup before taking stock of the whole picture.

Not bad. Not bad at all.

She slid her feet into her heels and donned her coat.

The space was already packed by the time she stepped through the doors.

Melinda Hanes was the front-runner for mayor, if for no other reason than her grandfather, father and brother had previously held the position. But it seemed that Nikki King had a lot of support. The atmosphere was exuberant.

Simone searched the throng for familiar faces. She felt, rather than saw, the moment Lance spotted her in the crowd.

A shiver slid up her spine, but this one was anything but fear. Awareness. Pure, unadulterated sexual awareness. She turned and locked eyes with him across the room. What she saw there made her stomach somersault.

He crossed the gallery to her. "Wow, you look spectacular."

His eyes raked over her, and for the first time in

her life, she knew what it meant to have a man undress her with his eyes.

Heat spread through her chest. "Oh, um…thank you. You too. I mean you look nice too."

Better than nice. She'd mostly seen him in his uniform, and while he looked good in it, she preferred his current attire. His dark slacks molded to muscular legs while the navy sports coat he'd thrown over a white button-down accentuated his broad shoulders and toned frame. Lance Webb was undeniably sexy.

He flashed a wicked grin at her. "You want to cut out of here and go back to your place?"

She absolutely did. "I can't. I'm working."

"That does not look like a work dress."

"Lance." A blush heated her cheeks. The compliment set her off balance. Not that he'd never complimented her before, but flirting with Lance out in public was a new experience. One she could get used to but probably shouldn't, given their arrangement.

She cleared her throat and took a step back out of his gravitational pull. "Have you heard from the medical examiner yet? Did he make an official ruling on how Holly Moyer died?"

Lance frowned. "You know I can't answer that. I know you're still working, but for the next couple of hours I'm off the clock."

She nodded. For the moment, she'd set the murder on the back burner, but that didn't mean she'd give up on getting more information out of him.

Lance smiled. "So how about I get you a drink?"

"Water would be nice."

They wound their way through the throng of people to the bar. Lance requested two mineral waters from the bartender and handed one to her.

She took a sip and let it cool her desire for the man in front of her. "It looks like Ms. King has quite a bit of support."

"Yeah, a lot of people have had it with the entire Hanes family."

"You included?"

It was no secret that there was no love lost between Lance and the current mayor, Melinda Hanes. He'd arrested Melinda's brother for fraud and embezzlement, and it was something the mayor was not willing to forgive or forget.

"Let's just say I'd like to see new blood in the mayor's office."

"Can I quote you on that?"

"Absolutely not. Officially, I'm neutral. I'm just here for the mineral water. And the company." He winked.

"So," he said, leading her away from the bar. "I know nothing about art. How about you?"

"I bet you know more than I do. I mean, what is this supposed to be?" She motioned toward a large canvas that appeared to be nothing more than blotches in various shades of gray.

Lance dipped his head to look at the printed information card mounted on the wall next to the canvas. "Well, according to this, it is supposed to be twenty thousand dollars."

The sip of water she'd just taken caught in her throat, sending her into a coughing fit.

Lance patted her back while she fought to stop the coughing.

"You caught me off guard. Twenty thousand dollars? For blobs of gray paint?"

"Art is in the eye of the beholder."

"And the beholder has a great big bank account, I guess."

Lance chuckled. "If he wants this piece, yes. This isn't one of James's."

She was grateful to get away from the expensive painting. Just standing in front of it made her nervous. What if she tripped and fell into it? Or someone bumped her hand and she spilled mineral water all over it? She didn't think everything she'd ever owned in her whole life totaled twenty thousand dollars and she was including the old hatchback she drove.

"James focuses on hyperrealistic drawings," Lance continued. "Drawings that look like they could be photographs. They really are quite amazing. I think… Yeah, here."

"The Valley of the Kings," she said, looking at the painting.

Lance glanced at the placard next to the drawing. "You're right. Have you been?"

"To Egypt? I wish. No, I just really like African history and culture. My dream trip would be a month just touring the continent and it wouldn't be long enough to see all the historically significant sites and gorgeous landscapes. The Valley of the Kings is home to sixty-three tombs, the burial site of a number of Egyptian pharaohs. All of the tombs are lavishly decorated. Videos and photographs aren't allowed on the site, so your James must have done this—"

"On-site."

She and Lance turned to find James West standing behind them. Simone had seen him a handful of times around town but had never been formally introduced. To say that up close he cut an intimidating figure was a gross understatement.

"And in hundred-degree weather since I made the foolish decision to visit during the summer months. I will not make that mistake twice." James West's smile was almost as devastating as Lance's.

"Lance. Simone. I'm so glad you could make it tonight."

"I wouldn't have missed it," Simone said. "I'm doing a write-up of the event for the *Weekly*, but I've been meaning to check out the gallery for a while now. I've heard wonderful things about your work. Compliments that are well deserved from what I can see."

Erika strolled to a stop next to her husband, her arms wrapping around his waist. James slung his arm around her shoulders and pulled her in closer. It was evident to anyone in the room these two were a unit, one that loved and respected each other.

What would it be like to have that kind of intimacy with someone? She slid another sidelong look at Lance.

The four of them chatted about James's art for a moment before they were interrupted by the crackle of a microphone. After a brief introduction by her campaign manager, Nikki King took the mic. She spoke with humor and warmth about growing up in Carling Lake, and her desire to see the town thrive and prosper struck Simone as genuine and sincere.

Voting hadn't been high on Simone's list of priorities, but Nikki might be worth the effort. She was one who really cared about the people she was asking to serve.

Nikki ended her remarks, and when the applause finally died down, Lance whispered in Simone's ear, "Can we get out of here now?"

His breath tickled her ear and sent butterflies fluttering in her stomach. "Someone might see us if we leave together."

The corners of her lips tipped up. "I have enough for my story. Meet you at my place in twenty?"

She headed for the coat check. She made the ten-minute walk to her apartment in half the time.

She trudged up the stairs and unlocked the apartment door, pushing it open and pausing in the door frame.

Someone had been inside her apartment. She couldn't give voice to how she knew—it was a feeling, a presence hanging over the space.

Then her eyes focused on the top of her dining room table.

A playing card with a skull lay on its surface. The word *cowardice* was penned in bloodred ink.

Simone stumbled back out of the apartment, fumbling in her purse for her phone as she hurried down the stairs and outside. Lance answered on the first ring.

"I just left the gallery," he said without preamble, his tone flirtatious.

"Lance—" Her words caught on a knot in her throat. She took a deep breath and started again. "I… I need you. Someone broke into my apartment."

"I'm two minutes away. Are you okay?"

"I'm fine. I'm in front of the building. Lance, I think it was the Card Killer."

THE KILLER WATCHED Simone's apartment from a safe distance, hidden in the shadows between buildings. He saw the sheriff race down the street on foot and dash into the vestibule of his lover's building. Oh, they'd taken pains to keep their torrid affair a secret, but he knew everything that went on in his town. He took pride in knowing who the reprobates in town were. He'd let his side project of getting rid of the worst of them fall to the side twenty years ago, but it felt good to be doing what was needed to keep the town the wholesome, family-oriented place it should be.

Sheriff Lance Webb sure wasn't up to the job. Although he did seem mighty protective of one of the town residents in particular.

Too bad his efforts would be futile.

He couldn't have been more surprised when he realized who Simone Jarrett was. The night he'd killed Nancy Oliver was the only time he'd feared being caught. He'd spent days in a cold sweat, waiting for the knock on his door that announced his end. But it had never come. He'd almost convinced himself that he hadn't seen the little girl running away from the woods.

But here she was, all grown up.

If she'd heeded his text warning her to back off, he might never have realized who she was. But she hadn't and he was almost thankful. It felt like they were coming full circle somehow.

Like his killing Simone Jarrett was always meant to be.

But doing so would require patience if he didn't want to get caught. Luckily, he hadn't gotten away with multiple murders for over two decades without having a deep well of patience.

The killer looked up at the windows of Simone's apartment, imagining what she and the sheriff were doing inside. Was she scared? Was the sheriff comforting her? He'd probably try to lift fingerprints from the apartment and the playing card he'd left.

Good luck with that.

He was not only patient, but he was also careful. They wouldn't find anything he didn't want them to find.

He stepped deeper into the shadows and turned away from Simone's building, walking toward his car.

It wasn't time yet, but soon.

Simone might be the sheriff's plaything now, but soon he'd entrap her in his web.

And she'd be his.

Chapter Twelve

Lance broke every traffic law in the books getting to Simone. He found her huddled in the alcove at the bottom of the stairs leading to her apartment.

He pulled her into his arms, not caring who might see them through the glass front door of the building.

"Are you alright?"

Her face was pale and fear showed in her eyes, but he couldn't see any physical injuries.

"I'm fine. There's a… Someone left a skull card on my dining room table."

He immediately went on high alert, pulling her back farther into the alcove and placing himself between her and whoever might be upstairs.

"Stay here," he commanded, drawing his gun from its holster and heading up the steps.

The apartment's door was open, but it didn't appear that it had been forced. The spare key was under the fire extinguisher. The intruder must have used it. He'd warned Simone about leaving it there, but she didn't want him hanging around in the hall if she was running late for their date nights.

Who else knew where she kept her spare key?

The living room, dining area and kitchen were visible in a quick sweep of the space. The only thing that looked out of place was the playing card on the dining table.

His stomach clenched in fury at the thought that someone had not only violated Simone's space but was threatening her as well. He pushed the feeling away and proceeded to clear the apartment.

The coat closet next to the door was tidy and clear of any intruders. He made his way to the bedroom door, checking the tiny bathroom before he stepped inside. Like the other parts of the apartment, there wasn't much to the room. A bed, dresser, nightstand and another closet that was also empty except for clothes and shoes. There was a laptop on the bed and two books on the night table, both popular thrillers. Whoever was threatening Simone—because the skull card in her dining room could be taken no other way—was gone.

He walked back into the living area. Through the open door, he could see her waiting in the hall.

"It's all clear," he said.

Simone stepped into the apartment, her eyes darting around as if she wasn't sure she believed him.

He took her hand and led her to the sofa. "Sit, but don't touch anything. Simone, it doesn't look like the lock on the door has been tampered with. Where's your spare key?"

"In the kitchen drawer."

He was happy to hear that for her safety, but instinct told him that there was more to the story. "You didn't put it back under the extinguisher?"

She swallowed. "No, you were right about it not being safe and…"

"And what?"

"Yesterday, before I found you in my shower, I received a text. I thought it was just someone trying to get me to drop my story. One of the victim's relatives."

"Can I see it?"

She dug her phone out of her bag and pulled up the text.

BACK OFF IF YOU KNOW WHAT'S GOOD FOR YOU.

He understood why she might not have taken the text too seriously at first. It wasn't threatening on its own, but taken in context with the current situation, he wasn't willing to be as dismissive of it as she'd been.

"I'm going to need to do a trace on your incoming calls."

She nodded.

He sat next to her on the sofa. "Why didn't you tell me about this?"

"It's not unusual for me to get vague threats. Not since I moved to Carling Lake, sure, but my stories often bring me in contact with people who don't want me to write about them."

"And this story has brought you in contact with someone like that? The person you assume sent this text?"

She chewed her bottom lip. "I talked to Ernestine Parks yesterday. Juanita Byers's sister. Her nephew, Juanita's son, Brian, showed up and he was not at all happy that I was writing about his mother's murder. But he would have been a child when his mother was murdered. He can't be the killer."

"He couldn't have killed anyone twenty years ago. We haven't ruled out Holly's murder as a copycat. And even if Brian isn't the killer, it doesn't mean he didn't send this text or break in here. Maybe Brian figured he could piggyback off the killer's modus operandi and scare you away."

Either way, he'd be paying Brian a visit soon. But right now his main concern was Simone.

"I'm going to call my deputy and have him come over to bag the card as evidence and dust for prints."

She sat, but he noted her skittishness. He'd only ever seen confident, collected Simone. Or Simone in the throes of passion. This Simone, unsure and visibly terrified, worried him.

He kept one eye on her while he crossed to the table and inspected the card. Because he couldn't risk touching it and destroying any fingerprints, though he doubted he'd find any, he pulled out his phone and took several pictures. He enlarged one of the pictures, studying every inch of it, but there was nothing visible that seemed to be of any use to him. It looked like the one they'd found with Holly's body except for the word *cowardice*.

Could this be the killer sending a message? But what? Simone was as far from a coward as anyone he'd ever met. And if the card had been left by the killer, it marked a deviation from his usual modus operandi.

Simone was still alive.

He glanced over at the woman who'd taken up residence in his heart. She was currently pacing a tight circle in front of the sofa. Abject fear stabbed at him at the thought of losing her. He couldn't let it happen. He *wouldn't* let it happen.

He placed the call to Bridges, filling him in quickly on the situation and the need for an evidence tech at Simone's address. They'd run the card for fingerprints, but he didn't have high hopes.

Ending the call, he turned back to Simone, his concern growing with each step she took.

He stepped back over to the sofa. "Maybe we should get you checked out at the hospital."

"No! I just need to leave."

"Okay, we can step outside while we wait for the evidence technician."

"No, I mean leave Carling Lake."

The words hit him like a sucker punch. "What? Where would you go?"

"I don't know. It doesn't matter. I just have to get out of Carling Lake. I should have never moved back here."

Moved back? What was she talking about?

She moved to go past him, but he shifted, blocking her way.

"You need to calm down. Think things through. Sit. I'm going to get you some water."

He went to the refrigerator, keeping one eye on her, concerned that she might bolt for the door while his back was turned. He grabbed a bottle of water, his thoughts ajumble.

I should have never moved back here.

Which meant she'd lived in Carling Lake before? When? It had to have been before he moved to town or he'd remember her, but if so, why had she kept it a secret?

He uncapped the bottle and pushed it into her hands. "Drink."

She took a sip.

He sat beside her on the sofa. "Okay, now what did you mean you shouldn't have come back?"

"Nothing. I just really need for you to leave. I've got to go."

It didn't escape him that she hadn't answered his question.

"Why? I get that what's happened here is scary, but don't you think that leaving town is extreme? I can't help feeling there's more to this than you're telling me."

Her gaze fell to the bottle in her hands.

The idea of Simone leaving Carling Lake and never seeing her again twisted his insides. He pushed the feeling away to deal with at another time. Right now he needed to find out why the card on her table had resulted in such an extreme reaction from her and who she believed had put it there.

Several moments passed. On the bright side, it appeared as if some of her initial fear and hysteria had passed, but she wasn't any more inclined toward opening up to him.

Their personal relationship aside, she clearly knew something about his case. He had to press.

"Simone, you need to tell me what you meant. A crime has been committed here. Someone broke into your apartment. Left an obviously threatening message for you that appears to be connected to a murder." He covered her hand with his. "Let me help you."

After a long moment, she nodded nearly imperceptibly. "Okay. I'll tell you everything."

Chapter Thirteen

Simone let out a breath she felt as if she'd been holding for twenty years. Dredging up memories of the night she'd seen Nancy Oliver killed, the night her entire life had drastically and irrevocably changed, wasn't something she wanted to do, but it was time.

She set the bottle of water on the coffee table and grabbed a pillow, hugging it to her like a shield. What would Lance think of her after she told him what she'd done? Would he look at her with contempt in his eyes? Would he think she was exactly what that card said? A coward. She twisted her hands in her lap and forced herself to go back to that horrible night.

"My mother and I lived in Carling Lake for a short time when I was twelve years old."

She caught the surprise that flashed in his eyes but kept going. "I've never told anyone and no one seemed to recognize me when I got back to town six months ago, probably because we lived here for less than a year. More like a stopover. One of many."

She reached for the water bottle and took a drink.

Talking about her childhood was almost as difficult as talking about that night.

"My mother was not what anyone would have called a stable person. We moved a lot. She was always looking for the next best thing. Which usually meant the next man willing to take care of her. Us. When she'd break up with whatever guy she was seeing at the moment, we'd move to a new town for a fresh start." She made air quotes around the last two words and let all the bitterness she felt about being shuttled from town to town pour through.

Lance squeezed her hand. "That sounds tough for a kid. I'm sorry you had to go through that."

"Yeah, me too. Anyway, the relationship with Kyle something, my mother's boyfriend at the time, was on its last legs. After years of living the pattern, I knew it well. They were arguing a lot, and on that night, they were so loud there was no way I'd get to sleep, so I slipped out of my bedroom window and went for a walk."

His eyebrows knit together. "At twelve you were wandering the streets at night. Even in Carling Lake…"

She held up her hand. "I know, and if I had a kid who pulled that, I'd ground them until they were out of college. But I already told you, my mother wasn't winning any parenting awards."

He held up his hands. "Sorry."

She sighed. It wasn't his fault she'd had a crappy childhood. "No, I'm procrastinating. I should get to the point."

He rubbed his thumb over the back of her hand. "Take your time."

"We lived in a place over on the bad side of Route 7. I know there isn't a bad side now that the city revitalization plan has allowed investors to improve the area, but twenty years ago it wasn't like that. The house we rented was a block from the wooded area that's still there." She swallowed hard and pulled her hand from his, needing space to say the next part. "I was walking along the edge of the trees, and when I got to the path, I saw a woman stumbling along like she was drunk. I recognized her as one of the women who shared a house down the street from my mom and me. I was about to turn back for home when a man stepped out of the trees onto the path. He wrapped something around the woman's neck and… I just froze."

She looked at Lance's face, trying to read what he was thinking, but his expression gave nothing away.

"I knew he was choking her, strangling her, but I couldn't make myself move or speak."

"You were a kid. You were scared."

"I was terrified. I screamed for help but the storm was too loud. I should have done more, but I just stood there, frozen. And then Nancy, later I learned her name was Nancy Oliver, went limp, and the man turned. I ran then. I ran home. I wanted to tell my mother what I'd seen. To call the police."

"But?"

A bitter laugh erupted from her throat. "She wasn't there. I fell asleep on the couch waiting for her to come home, and when she did at ten o'clock the next morning, I told her what I'd seen and that I needed to go to the police."

The look he gave her was knowing. "But she didn't take you."

"No. She said I'd just dreamed it. And when I swore that I hadn't, she said it wasn't our business. That if I went to the police, they'd think she or I had something to do with it. That I'd get in trouble for not calling the cops right away."

"That's not true."

"I know that now, but as you said, I was a kid. When they found Nancy's body, I was terrified. I just wanted it to go away. The next week, my mother packed up our things and we moved to a new town. I tried to forget what I'd seen, but Nancy and the nightmare of what I saw that night has plagued me for the last twenty years."

"So that's why you came back to Carling Lake?"

She nodded. "When I saw the posting for the position at the *Weekly*, it seemed like fate. With the anniversary of the murders coming up, I thought maybe if I could reinvigorate interest in the case, the killer could finally be brought to justice."

His eyes darkened with displeasure and maybe even a hint of revulsion. "Why didn't you report what you'd seen twenty years ago when you came back to town? All the time we've spent together in the last several months. Why haven't you said anything to me?"

There it was. The judgment she'd been so terrified of hearing in his voice.

She pushed to her feet. "Because of the look on your face right now. Because that card is right. I'm a coward."

He stood too, his face softening. "Simone—"

"No, I saw the disgust in your eyes. I get it. I've been an adult for years now. Maybe not saying anything was excusable when I was a kid, but what about the last decade or so?" She stopped his movement toward her with an outstretched hand. "How could I expect people not to judge me for keeping what I saw to myself when I judge myself? Every. Single. Day."

"You shouldn't. Nobody should judge you," he said warily. "You witnessed something traumatic as a child and that trauma doesn't just go away because you grew up."

Silence washed over them.

"So what now?"

Lance's forehead furrowed in thought. "You said Nancy's killer turned. Could he have seen you?"

"I didn't think so. Or at least I didn't want to let myself think he did. But in my recurring nightmare about the murder, when I start to run home, a man steps out of the shadows and reaches for me."

Lance nodded. "So it's possible he saw you and your subconscious knows it."

She crossed her hands over her chest protectively. "I guess it's possible. I've had that dream, nightmare really, two or three times a week for the last twenty years."

He dipped his head and looked her in the eye, his

expression thoughtful. "We've spent the night together dozens of times in the last few months. How
come I didn't know that?"

Her heart rate picked up, but she held his gaze.
"Because I never have the dream when you're in bed
next to me."

She held her breath, waiting for his reaction. Maybe
it was one reveal too many, but it was the truth. His
presence somehow quelled the nightmares. She
couldn't explain it, or rather she hadn't let herself think
about it long enough to devise an explanation for it.
At least not with words. Whether her heart knew was
another thing altogether.

The sound of the door opening off the street one
floor below startled her.

Lance stepped in front of her and pressed a soft
kiss to her lips. "It's just the evidence tech on her way
up. I'll let her in and you go pack a bag. You can stay
with me for a few nights."

He moved around her to the still open door.

Her head throbbed, the physical result of the emotional grinder she'd been through in the last hour. Now
that her initial flight instinct had passed, she agreed
with Lance that leaving Carling Lake would've been
a knee-jerk overreaction. She'd come back to this
town on a mission to help find a killer, and if Lance's
theory was correct, she was succeeding better than
she'd anticipated.

And she couldn't deny that the idea of moving in
with him, even if it was only into his guest room, was

tempting. Lately, it had become more and more difficult to stop herself from falling into daydreams of a real future between the two of them. But that was all they were—silly dreams. Especially since he now knew the secret she'd been keeping from him. She couldn't forget the reproach she'd seen in his eyes moments earlier.

She wasn't going to run this time. Not from Carling Lake and not from her apartment. Twenty years was long enough to be scared. She was going to stay, but on her terms.

She waited for Lance to finish giving instructions to his tech. "I'm not leaving. Carling Lake or my home. I'm staying here tonight."

He frowned. "I don't think that's a good idea. Not until we can beef up the security around here. The killer may know you saw him murder Nancy Oliver."

"I'm not asking for permission. This is my home and I won't be run out of it."

Lance massaged his forehead with one hand. "Simone, I'm happy you aren't leaving town, but you have to think about your safety. Staying here when we know someone, someone potentially very dangerous, knows how to get inside the apartment is not safe."

"I appreciate your concern, but as soon as you are finished collecting your evidence, I'm calling a locksmith and having the locks changed. I'll be fine." She walked to the open apartment door, underscoring the finality of her decision.

Taking the hint, Lance followed her to the door.

The frown on his face deepened. "I think you're making a mistake."

She fixed her gaze on his brown eyes and fortified her resolve. "It's my mistake to make."

Chapter Fourteen

A three-hundred-dollar emergency locksmith visit and a sleepless night left Simone more than a little cranky at the knock that came on her door at seven the next morning. Expecting to find Lance, she was still pleasantly surprised when she opened the door to Erika West, two cups of coffee and a baker's box of fresh Danish.

Erika bustled into the apartment dressed in a T-shirt, blue yoga pants and running shoes. "I heard about the break-in. I figured you could use some morning cheer. Sorry about the early hour, but I can't stay long. I have to get back to the B and B."

"If that's a cinnamon latte I smell, I'm willing to forgive you anything," Simone said, turning the brand-new bolt on the door to lock it before joining Erika at the table.

"It is. I didn't know whether you liked cinnamon or pumpkin spice, so I got one of each."

"Either. Both. Beggars can't be choosers and I am definitely a beggar this morning. I didn't get any sleep last night."

"I bet. I can't believe someone broke into your apartment."

"They didn't just break in." Simone sipped her coffee.

Erika's eyebrow went up. "No?"

"They also left a calling card. Literally. Left a card with the skull design."

Erika's eyes widened. "Like the one found with the body of that poor woman the other day?"

"Exactly. And like the ones found with the victims of the Card Killer twenty years ago."

"That's unbelievable. Terrifying."

She wasn't sure why, but she felt as if she needed to tell Erika the whole truth. Maybe because she was the closest thing to a real girlfriend Simone had in Carling Lake. Maybe it was just easier since she'd told Lance already, but the words were out before she had a chance to think about it too much. "I was there when Nancy Oliver was murdered."

Simone launched into the rest of the story without giving Erika a chance to react to what she'd just said.

When she was finished, Erika shifted her chair from the opposite end of the table to Simone's side and grasped her hand. "I am so sorry you had to go through that. What can I do to help?"

Simone squeezed her friend's hand. "You just did it." She breathed out a sigh of relief. "I told Lance everything yesterday after the break-in. He thinks the killer may have seen me twenty years ago and is targeting me now because I may be able to identify him."

Erika quirked an eyebrow. "Can you?"

She shook her head. "No. All I saw was a figure in the shadows. I'm sure it was a man, but beyond that…"

Erika leaned back in her chair. "Well, that does explain why Lance is parked outside your building so early in the morning." She shot her a pointed look. "My guess is he's been there all night."

Erika's statement caused Simone to choke on the coffee she'd just taken a sip of. It took a moment to get the coughing under control. "What?"

Erika wore a mischievous smile.

"Sheriff Webb. Looks like he slept in his car in front of your apartment last night, I assume, to make sure you're safe." She wiggled her eyebrows.

Simone rose and glanced out of the window over-looking the street. A sheriff's department SUV was parked illegally in front of the building.

"Why don't you take him this cup of coffee." Erika held up the second cup she'd brought over but hadn't touched. "It's probably cold, but if Lance slept in the car, he won't care. And invite him in for a Danish. There's plenty."

She took the coffee and pushed her feet into sneakers before heading out the door. It was a warm morning, thankfully, since she hadn't bothered to throw on a robe over her cotton pajama set.

She stepped out of the building and Lance let down the driver's-side window as she rounded the front of the SUV.

Despite the shadow of stubble around his jaw and the dark circles under his eyes, he looked…good.

"I brought you coffee," she said, extending the cup. "It's cold though."

"Thanks." Lance pulled the coffee into the car through the open window. "Why don't you hop in the other side?"

She rounded the car and got in. "What are you doing here?"

Lance took a sip of coffee and looked at her guilelessly. "What do you mean?"

"I didn't know the sheriff's department provided private protection."

"It doesn't. I'm off the clock." He smiled and took another sip.

"Don't you think sleeping in your car is a bit of overkill?"

"You wouldn't listen to reason about staying here."

"I had the locks changed. Nothing happened. I was perfectly safe."

"Maybe. Or maybe nothing happened because you had the sheriff sitting outside your apartment all night. We'll never know."

"So this is your plan. You're going to camp out in front of my apartment every night."

"I do like sleeping in your bed a lot better than sleeping in front of your building. But we all do what we must."

She touched his hand but wouldn't meet his gaze. "And I like having you in my bed." There was so much more to say, but she wasn't sure how.

He reached across the space between them and

tipped her chin up so her eyes met his. "I'm scared for you."

"I'm sorry I didn't tell you the truth from the beginning. We were keeping things casual, but then it seemed like things weren't as casual anymore. I wasn't sure how you'd react."

"How do you want me to react?"

"I... I'm not sure."

His eyes clouded. She could tell he didn't like that answer, but it was the truth. So much had happened in the last couple of days. The world felt like it was shifting under her feet and she wasn't sure how she felt or if what she felt was real or just a reaction to all the change.

He took his hand away and faced forward. "Okay."

She wasn't sure she was ready to delve into what that "okay" meant, but she was saved from having to at the moment. Erika tapped on Simone's window. "Are you two coming inside or what? I warmed the Danish."

Lance leaned forward and smiled at Erika through the glass before focusing a pointed gaze back on Simone. "I could eat something. That is if you'll let me back into your apartment."

Simone threw her hands up in a gesture of surrender. "Sure. Come on in. The more the merrier, I guess."

They both got out of the SUV and followed Erika back up to the apartment. Like the superb B and B owner and hostess that she was, Erika had set the table and laid the now warm Danish on a serving plate. A pot of hot coffee brewed in the coffee maker.

Erika's phone rang before she sat down. "Oh, I have to take this. Give me a minute."

"You can take it in my bedroom if you need privacy." Simone tilted her head toward the corridor leading to her bedroom.

"Thanks." Erika turned and disappeared down the hall.

Simone poured two fresh cups of coffee for herself and Erika and carried them to the dining room table, where Lance already sat eating his Danish. Since she hadn't been able to sleep, she'd spent a good chunk of the night thinking about her article and the possibility that the Card Killer was back. She'd returned to Carling Lake looking for justice and she was resolved to do whatever she could to get it.

"I have a proposition for you," she said.

He looked at her with one eyebrow cocked upward in question.

"Let's work together."

He wiped his mouth with a napkin before saying, "No way."

"We are probably going to be talking to a lot of the same people. You for your investigation and me for the *Weekly*. What's the harm?"

"The harm is investigating crimes is my job, not yours. The harm is that someone has already broken into your apartment and left a threat."

"Exactly. I'm already a target for someone. It seems

to me that the faster we figure out who, the safer I'll be. And since two heads are better than one…"

"This is an insane idea. You need to drop it."

She met his gaze directly. "I can be of help to you. I already spoke to one of Holly's coworkers, who told me that another coworker and Holly were friends. I'd planned to track down this friend yesterday, but the break-in derailed that plan."

"What friend? I had deputies speak to everyone on staff at the Fairmont and every one of them said Holly wasn't particularly close to anyone there."

"Arianna Arjan. She works at the Fairmont and was somewhat of a teacher's pet to Holly. And you've proved my point. People don't like to talk to cops. They will talk to me. Let me help you."

Lance studied her.

She raced on. "I also learned that Holly might have been having an affair with her boss. Which would give Fred Knauer a motive to kill Holly if the relationship turned sour. I still have to talk to Knauer, but…"

"He's not a suspect. He has an alibi."

"Oh." She frowned. "I guess you already knew about the affair. But you didn't know about Arianna. I did help you there. You have to admit, people are willing to tell me things that they might not want to tell you."

"I admit nothing."

She met his gaze directly. "I'm going to chase this story no matter what."

He glowered silently, but she could see he was considering what she'd said.

"On one condition. You stay in my guest room until this is all sorted out."

She was shaking her head before he finished the sentence. "I... I can't."

"Look, if you want to put our relationship on hold or even end it..." His Adam's apple bobbed.

"I didn't say that."

"I might not have handled things the best way last night, but—"

"I think you handled it pretty well, all things considered. I think we have a lot to work out, but right now..."

"Right now there's a killer on the loose and you have a story to write. I get it. And I'm genuinely just offering you a safe place to stay, no expectations."

"You may not have expectations, but this is a small town, and once people find out I'm shacked up with the sheriff... Whatever we ultimately decide we are or aren't, it doesn't need the pressure of us living under the same roof."

Lance's expression darkened. "Simone, this is about your safety."

Erika stepped out of the bedroom. "Sorry if I'm interrupting. Is everything okay?" She looked from Simone to Lance.

"Everything is fine," Simone answered.

"Everything is not fine," Lance said pointedly. "I'm trying to convince her that staying here isn't safe. Yes, the lock has been changed," he offered before she could, "but the intruder got in without a key the last time, so we can't be sure he won't be able to do it again even with new locks. I've offered to let her have my guest room."

Erika's mouth turned up into a sly smile, which was all the more reason that Simone was sure that she couldn't stay with Lance. The moment this town found out she'd spent the night at his place, even under the circumstances, the rumor mill would go into overdrive. That would be the end of their secret casual affair. Although from the smile on Erika's face, it may not have been as secret as they thought. But Erika suspecting something was going on between them was one thing. Simone trusted her to be discreet. Others in town? Not so much.

Simone returned Lance's pointed stare. "And I was just explaining to the sheriff that staying with him would be inappropriate."

"Simone, I don't give a fig about inappropriate right now. I have a guest room and a state-of-the-art security system at my house."

She planted her hands on her hips. "Well, bully for you. I do give a fig because it's my journalistic integrity that would be called into question—"

"May I make a suggestion?" Erika interrupted. "I run a B and B. I've got plenty of rooms open right now and the place is a fortress. With a burly former marine standing guard."

Simone had to admit it wasn't a bad idea. She didn't love Lance presuming that she'd leave her home, but she wasn't blind to the fact that someone had gotten into the apartment and they weren't sure how. Not to mention that even with the new locks, she'd been too afraid to sleep a wink.

"I'm willing to stay at the B and B for a couple of nights. Just until I get a security system to go with the new locks on the door," Simone conceded.

Lance nodded. "I can live with that."

"I'll also need an exclusive interview with you when you catch the killer."

His frown deepened. "*If* I catch the killer."

She looked into his eyes. "I have faith in you." A charged moment passed between them. "We have a deal?"

Lance nodded again. "Deal."

She beat back the urge to do a celebratory jig, but just barely. "I need to stop by the *Weekly* and update Aaron."

"And I need to go home to shower and change. Why don't you meet me at the sheriff's station when you finish with Aaron? We can speak to Arianna Arjan together."

Erika clapped her hands. "Wonderful. Simone, if you pack a bag I can take it back to the B and B with me and have it waiting for you in your room when you arrive."

"That would be great." Simone smiled at her friend.

Hopefully, her exclusive with Lance would help her keep her job when she told Aaron about her connection to Nancy Oliver.

AARON TOOK THE revelation that she had witnessed Nancy Oliver's murder much better than Simone expected. He sat behind his desk, while Margaret sat in the chair beside Simone and Kate stood back by the office door. Even with her back to the young woman, Simone could feel her hanging on every word.

"I don't know what to say," Aaron said in a voice more shocked than angry.

"I realize that I promised not to keep anything else from you, but I only told Sheriff Webb last night. It was the first time I'd ever spoken about what I saw to anyone except my mother."

"Oh, honey. We understand. It must have been awful for you," Margaret answered, patting Simone's back sympathetically.

"I think it would be best if I took over reporting on the Holly Moyer murder and the Card Killer anniversary piece," Aaron said.

"No!" Simone cried out. "Aaron, you can't. I can still write this story."

Aaron shook his head. "Your objectivity…"

Simone slid to the end of the chair she was sitting in. Margaret pulled her hand back onto her lap.

"I can still be objective. What I saw all those years ago motivates me, yes, but that is useful. I will not stop until I get to the bottom of this crime."

Aaron snorted. "That is exactly what I'm afraid of. Your apartment has been broken into and you said you received a text you think could be from the killer. I have to consider your safety."

"You don't have to worry about that. I made a deal with Sheriff Webb. He has agreed to work together and to give me an exclusive interview after he's caught the killer in exchange for me staying at Erika West's B and B for a few nights. And you know that property is well protected."

Aaron's brow furrowed. "That doesn't seem like much of a deal for the sheriff."

Margaret coughed conspicuously. Simone shared a look with Aaron's wife. Her pointed gaze was enough to let Simone know that her relationship with Lance had not gone as unnoticed as she'd thought. She had to wonder how many others in town suspected something was going on between them.

"Be that as it may, it is a good deal for us. Simone has an inside track on the case, and she will be with the sheriff, so that should allay any safety concerns."

"And I could help." Kate stepped forward. "With research and fact-checking anything that might raise concerns about Simone's objectivity. Even help with the writing. For a byline of course."

Since she had already pegged Kate as smart and ambitious, Simone wasn't surprised to see the young reporter jump on the opportunity for her first byline at the *Weekly*. She actually admired it. She'd acted similarly when she was a young, hungry new reporter trying to break into the business.

She smiled and nodded Kate's way to let her know she was on board.

Aaron didn't look convinced, but he conceded. "But I need to know every single move you are making on this."

"Absolutely." Simone stood and made to leave the office before he changed his mind.

"Simone." Aaron's voice had her turning around before she walked out of the door. "Be careful."

Kate followed Simone back to her desk.

"I have to meet Sheriff Webb. We're going to speak to one of Holly's friends." Simone scooped her laptop into her messenger bag.

"I think I should go with you," Kate said.

Simone shook her head. "I don't think the sheriff will let both of us ride along with him."

Kate narrowed her eyes. "You heard Aaron. I'm on this story now too. Officially. You can't shut me out."

Simone threw her phone into her bag and turned to Kate. "I'm sorry I haven't been as open to working with you as I should have been, but I promise I'm not shutting you out." She unsnapped her wristband and pulled back the flap covering the flash drive. "Here. All my notes are on this."

Kate took the wristband, turning it over in her hand with a look of surprise. "That's so cool."

Simone's eyes tracked back to Aaron's office. He watched her and Kate, a veiled expression in his eyes. She had to prove to him she could still get this story right.

She focused back on Kate. "Get familiar with the information on it. See if I've missed anything and, if so, run down whatever you think I should have. Keep me in the loop. Do not take any chances or do anything risky."

"Got it." Kate beamed.

"We'll regroup after I'm finished with the sheriff." Simone headed for the elevators, feeling lighter than she had in years. Maybe going it alone had been the wrong choice. With a whole team now, she was sure to get justice for Nancy and the other victims of the Card Killer.

Chapter Fifteen

Lance took a quick shower and shaved when he arrived home. His back continued to protest his having spent the night sitting upright, but he'd do it again if he had to. Anything to make sure Simone was safe.

Their relationship aside, he genuinely believed Simone would be safest staying with him. That she didn't want to rankled him. Logically he understood where she was coming from. Once the town gossips got wind she was staying in his guest room, they'd talk. And talk. And talk some more. But so what? Maybe it was time to bring this thing between them out in the open. Yes, they'd have to work around the issues it posed for both their careers, but they weren't insurmountable.

He didn't love that she hadn't told him about witnessing Nancy Oliver's murder, but again he understood it. Fear made people do all sorts of things. He hadn't told her the details about why his marriage had ended, which was fine when he was sure he wanted to keep things casual. But now? Maybe they needed to have a heart-to-heart.

That was if she wanted to try. Over the last few weeks, he'd begun to think that they were building something real. Something lasting. But now he wasn't so sure.

Maybe that was for the best. He'd sworn off serious relationships after his marriage to Jen failed. That was over a decade ago and he'd been true to his word, never even considering taking a relationship past the casual phase, until now.

Maybe the universe was reminding him of his vow. He'd thought he was marriage material at one point in his life, but clearly he wasn't. Jen certainly wasn't, as evidenced by the multiple affairs she'd had after they'd failed at having a child. Jen hadn't thought he would be enough. Maybe Simone wouldn't either.

But now wasn't the time to delve into all this. His priorities had to be keeping Simone safe and finding Holly Moyer's killer. In that order. Erika wasn't wrong about her B and B being as close to a fortress as they were going to find in Carling Lake. Erika was married to James West, a former marine and part of the family who owned the elite firm West Security and Investigations. When Erika and her son had unexpectedly come into an inheritance to the tune of billions, James and his brothers had spared no expense outfitting the B and B with the best security available.

Simone would be safe there.

A thought popped into his head and he smiled, reaching for his phone.

"I have a favor to ask," Lance said when James

West answered the other end of the line. He explained what he wanted.

"Why do I think this is going to turn out badly?" James sighed.

"Will you do it?"

"I'll do it, but when it backfires, you're on your own."

"Fair enough."

"What is going on with you and Simone by the way? I don't make a habit of prying, but it's clear she means something to you. I'm just wondering how much."

"I'm working on figuring out the answer to that question," Lance said before hanging up.

He packed a bag and headed to the station. The first thing he did after arriving was pull his second-in-command, Deputy Clark Bridges, into his office and update him on the status of the case, Simone's status as a witness in Nancy Oliver's murder, and the threats against her. He couldn't force her to accept protection, but he could order Deputy Clarke to spread the word that his deputies were to keep an eye out and to increase patrols around the *Weekly* and her apartment building.

He finished briefing Deputy Clarke and did a cursory search for information on Arianna Arjan. The nineteen-year-old had graduated from high school a year ago and started working at the Fairmont Inn & Resort approximately nine months earlier. Her official title was "associate," which appeared to mean she manned the reception desk and did other odd jobs around the resort. The address on her driver's license was for a middle-class neighborhood in Stunnersville.

Simone texted to let him know she was on her way. He waited in front of the building and was more than a little irritated when he saw her turn the corner, walking toward him alone. The *Weekly*'s offices were only a few blocks away, but under the circumstances she'd have been safer driving than walking. Maybe he needed to stress, once again, the seriousness of the threats against her.

"I'll drive." He led her to his official vehicle.

During the ride, Simone filled him in on her meeting with Aaron and Margaret and the addition of Kate to the story.

"So our unlikely partnership has your boss's stamp of approval," Lance said without taking his eyes from the road.

"Yes." She hesitated. "There's something else. I think Margaret is aware of our relationship."

Lance glanced across the car. "It was probably wishful thinking, believing we could keep a secret in this town. And I'm not sure I want to keep trying to."

She turned and looked out of the side window silently for several moments. "Are you ending things?" she asked softly.

"No! That's not what I meant at all." He reached across the gearshift for her hand. "I want to go public with our relationship."

Simone let out a heavy breath. "I don't know."

"That's okay. This isn't the best time for this conversation anyway. Just… Will you think about it?" He looked over at her, catching her smile.

"Yeah, I'll think about it."

He squeezed her hand and turned his focus back to the case, as they reached Arianna's street.

He pulled to a stop in front of a modest clapboard house and turned to Simone. "Let me take the lead. My murder investigation trumps your article."

She held her hands up. "I can do that."

They exited the car and knocked on the door of the house. A woman with short gray hair wearing a housecoat opened the door. A dishrag hung over her shoulder and she glared at them through the screen.

"Can I help you?"

"My name is Sheriff Lance Webb and this is Simone Jarrett. Is Arianna home?"

The woman shot an uneasy glance between them. "What do you want with her?"

He hid his irritation with the woman behind a smile. "I just need to ask her a few questions."

"Mom, who's at the door?" A younger version of the woman peeked around the door.

"Go to your room," the older woman barked.

The younger woman scowled. "I'm not a child. You can't send me to my room."

"This is my house, and if I say go to your room, that's what you'll do."

"Ladies, please." Lance focused on the younger woman now. "Are you Arianna Arjan?"

The young woman looked at him with suspicion in her eyes. She was probably thinking she should have listened to her mother. "Yes," she answered cautiously.

"I'm Sheriff Webb. This is Simone Jarrett. Do you mind if we ask you some questions?"

"Is this about Holly?"

Lance smiled again. "Just a few questions. Please."

Arianna hesitated a moment, then pushed the screen door open and stepped outside.

The older woman said something in a language he didn't recognize but that needed no translation before disappearing farther into the house.

"I already answered a bunch of questions about Holly," Arianna said, eyeing Simone.

Lance pulled out his notebook. "I just have a few follow-up questions."

"Who is she?" Arianna jutted her chin at Simone.

"I'm a reporter for the *Carling Lake Weekly*."

Arianna took a step closer to Simone, her eyes lighting up. "Are you writing a story on Holly?"

"Maybe. Right now I'm just trying to get some background on who Holly was."

He'd have to explain in detail what letting him take the lead looked like when they returned to the car because this wasn't it. "Could we focus on my questions, please, ladies?"

Arianna gave a put-upon sigh. "What do you want to know?"

"Some of your coworkers seem to think that you and Holly Moyer were close."

Arianna's nose scrunched as if she'd smelled something foul. "Close? I don't know about that."

"Well, how would you describe it?"

"We worked together. That's all."

"Holly didn't maybe take a special interest in you?" Simone interjected. Lance shot a frown at her that she ignored. "Maybe you saw her as a mentor?"

Arianna snorted. "Not likely. Holly wasn't the mentor type."

"What type was she?" Lance asked.

"Look, I'm sure I'm not the first to tell you that Holly was a difficult person. She was the boss and she never let those of us who worked below her forget it."

"So she was tough to work for?"

"Impossible. Never satisfied. Always expecting us to work overtime without notice. Taking credit for our work. The only people she was nice to were the guests."

"I was told that she wasn't as hard on you," Simone said.

"I guess she was a little nicer to me. I kissed up to her a lot. Made me sick to my stomach sometimes, but I want to work my way up to hotel management, and having Holly on my side would have gone a long way."

"So you two were friendly," Lance said.

"I guess," Arianna said begrudgingly.

"Holly's driver's license says she lived in Stunnersville. Do you have any idea why she'd be in Carling Lake?"

Arianna shook her head.

Simone cleared her throat. "What about the rumor that Holly and the manager at the resort were having an affair."

The question drew another pointed look from Lance.

"That wasn't a rumor. That was a fact. Holly told me about it herself."

"She did?" Lance's eyebrows quirked up.

Arianna nodded. "She couldn't treat Fred like a serf, since he was her boss, so she did the next best thing to get him under her thumb."

"So she was using him," Simone said.

"Holly was only ever interested in people for what they could do for her. The affair with Fred gave her leverage over him. Stupid man."

If Knauer realized that Holly was playing him for a fool, he might have been angry enough to kill her. But that theory left a lot of loose ends. None of the theories he'd come up with so far in this case fit perfectly. It was frustrating.

"Did Fred know Holly was only using him?"

Arianna shrugged. "I have no idea. He was married, so he was using her too. Maybe they were both okay with it. I do know that he wasn't the only man Holly was seeing."

Simone bounced on the tip of her toes with excitement. "Who else was she seeing?"

"That I don't know. Holly wouldn't tell me his name, but she also wouldn't stop talking about how smart and rich the new guy was. I figured he must also be married, or why would she have to hide the relationship?"

That was one possibility, but he'd need a name to confirm it.

"Look, I have to get ready for my shift."

Lance handed Arianna his business card. "If you think of anything else, please give me a call."

She took the card but turned her gaze to Simone. "So are you going to use what I said in a story? 'Cause I'm okay with that, but I don't want my name used, okay?"

"I'm not sure yet, but I promise no names."

They bid farewell to Arianna and the young woman went back into the house.

"So what are you thinking?" Simone said when they were in the car and on the road back to Carling Lake.

"I've got to talk to Knauer again and try to track down this new boyfriend."

"I can help with that."

"How?"

"Social media of course. I've done a little digging around in Holly's online life, but I can have Kate dig around more. At her age, she's bound to be better at that kind of stuff than I am."

"If Holly was keeping the boyfriend secret, there might not be anything online."

Simone rolled her eyes. "She was keeping the boyfriend so secret that she told a coworker."

"Point taken. I'll drop you at the *Weekly*'s offices and you can get started on cyber sleuthing."

"That works for me."

He pressed the gas, sending the SUV shooting ahead faster. "Okay, partner. Let's get to work."

Chapter Sixteen

As soon as Simone got back to the *Weekly*'s offices, she got Kate started on scouring Holly's social media for any sign of a secret boyfriend. So far it appeared Kate was getting nowhere. If Holly had a secret boyfriend, she'd done a good job of keeping him secret. Especially since Holly was a woman who liked to post about her life. She had thousands of posts on Instagram and Facebook detailing her daily exercise routine, eating habits and various likes and dislikes. The Fairmont didn't attract A-list celebrities or even B-list celebrities, but Holly seemed to make sure to get and post a photo of herself with anyone with even a hint of fame who came to the resort. Simone compiled a list of names of Holly's friends and associates who might be worth talking to so the effort wasn't a complete waste of time.

Simone was also frustrated. She'd pulled as much information as she could on Holly from the various databases the *Weekly* had access to, but nothing jumped out as suspicious or likely to have contributed to the woman's murder. She'd gone through all the information she had on Nancy, Deborah and Juanita, looking for some link that might connect one or more of the women to Holly, and found nothing. Still, her gut was telling her that these women weren't randomly chosen by the killer. Although whatever the connection between the women was might only be in the killer's mind.

"Simone. Earth to Simone." She looked up, surprised to find Lance standing next to her desk.

"Hey. Sorry. I was engrossed."

"I could tell. Hi." Lance shot a smile over her head at Kate. "You must be Kate."

"I am. It's nice to finally meet you, Sheriff. I hear we'll be working together, kind of."

Lance's eyebrows arched.

Simone shot a quelling look at Kate. "I mentioned to the sheriff that you were helping me on the article, although your work will be more behind-the-scenes and in the office and not directly working with the sheriff."

"Of course," Kate said through pursed lips. "I'm going to get a fresh cup of coffee. Does anyone else want one?"

Lance and Simone declined and Kate strode away to the break room.

"A little office rivalry," Lance teased.

Simone sighed. "It's fine. She's got talent and fire and she does good work. That's all I care about."

"Speaking of, how's it going?"

"Eh. Not great."

"I haven't had a lot of success either. The Stunnersville police sent an officer to Holly's apartment to look for anything that might point us toward her secret boyfriend and came up with nothing."

"What about Holly's boss?"

"I called Fred Knauer when I returned to the station to request he come in for a formal interview. He reiterated he had nothing to do with the murder, declined to come in for the interview and then he clammed up. Said to contact his lawyer if I wanted to speak to him again."

"That's suspicious."

Lance shook his head. "Not really. He was having an affair with a woman who was murdered. His wife knows now, thanks to this investigation. He's angry. Blaming me for his life falling apart."

"True."

"I reached out to the next of kin for Nancy Oliver and Deborah Indigo. I hoped time may have knocked loose some information that could help us now. No one answered at either number though, so I have to wait until they get back to me."

Simone snorted. "Good luck. I think the cops have an even harder time getting callbacks than reporters."

"I was more successful with tracking down Brian Byers since he still lives in town. He works as an auto mechanic across town. I called and the receptionist told me he was getting off work in about a half hour. You want to come with me to talk to him?"

She wasn't in any hurry to spend time with Brian Byers, but she'd worked hard to convince Lance to let her help with the investigation and she wasn't going to duck the hard parts.

"Where you go, I go."

Something about the statement struck her as more intimate than she'd intended.

An awkward pall sliced the air between them.

"I just meant…yes. I would like to go with you to question Brian."

"Great. Then let's get moving. I don't want to miss him."

They arrived at the auto body shop as Brian was leaving through a side door. He was dressed in blue-and-white coveralls and carried a cloth lunch bag. His long dreads were pulled back into a bun at the nape of his neck, but his outfit was much the same as it had been when she'd met him at his aunt's house. He glowered when he spotted Simone and Lance approaching.

"Mr. Byers. Can we speak to you for a moment?" Lance said.

"I don't have time right now. I gotta be somewhere." Brian kept walking.

"It will just take a moment," Lance said firmly.

Brian stopped walking. For a moment he looked as if he might argue. "What do you want to ask about?"

"I'm sure you've heard about the recent murder and its possible connection to your mother and the other two women killed twenty years ago."

"Yeah. She—" Brian jerked a thumb in Simone's direction "—was harassing my aunt. Then I saw her article."

Simone frowned. She understood that Brian had suffered a tragedy losing his mother in such a horrible way while so young. But she just did not like the man. "I wasn't harassing your aunt. I was interviewing her. An interview she agreed to."

"Whatever," he snarled. "Just stay away from her."

"Mr. Byers, did you know Holly Moyer?"

"No. Never heard of her before she got herself killed."

Lance's brows knit together. "Can you take a look at this photo?" Lance pulled his phone from his pocket. "Maybe you've seen her around. Could she have brought her car here for service?"

"I said I don't know her. I work in the back. I don't meet the customers. Anyway, where was all this investigating when my mother was murdered? It's been twenty years and you cops still haven't found her killer. Y'all just forgot all about her."

"No one forgot about your mother or the other women killed. We just didn't have any new leads to follow."

Simone jumped in. "That's why I was interviewing your aunt. I'm writing an article about the murders in hopes that someone remembers something helpful and brings it to the police."

Lance slid his phone back into his pocket. "Brian, you know there's a possibility that the most recent murder is—"

"The Card Killer. If you cops had done your jobs years ago, this Holly woman might be alive."

Lance tensed but ignored the jab. "Mr. Byers, do

you remember anything about the day your mother was killed? Or the days right before?"

Brian laughed mirthlessly. "Are you kidding? I was six."

"What about since then? Maybe someone had mentioned something to you about that day or the days leading up to her murder?"

"Look, man, I don't know. I remember she was worried. Of course, I didn't know why then, but now I know she'd lost her job a couple of weeks earlier."

"At the pharmacy, right?" Simone chimed in.

Brian nodded. "Yeah. My mother's boss had it out for her. He blamed her for the missing money, but I know my mother would have never done such a thing."

"Anything else you can remember?" Lance asked.

"I told you, I was just a kid."

Lance handed Brian one of his business cards. "Okay, if you remember anything, please call."

Brian stuffed it into the pocket of his overalls without looking at it. "Yeah, sure."

Simone turned with Lance and headed for his SUV.

"Hey, there is one other thing I remember," Brian called out.

They turned and walked back to him.

"The…last time I saw her, Mom got a call. It was late and the phone ringing woke me up. The person on the other end of the call must have said something good because she squealed, happy-like. I remember because she'd been so sad all the time."

"Do you have any idea who the call was from?"

Brian shook his head. "No. I just know Mom went out after that call."

Simone's brows went up. "She left you at home alone?"

"She didn't do it often, but if she was just running to the corner store, she sometimes did."

"I don't remember seeing a call mentioned in any of the reports."

Brian's gaze shifted up to the blue sky as if in thought. "I don't know if I mentioned it to the cops then. They had a lady ask me questions about my mom, but mostly I just remember being sad and scared."

As much as Simone didn't like Brian Byers, her heart went out to him at that moment.

"Do you know if your mother was dating anyone at the time?" she asked. It was a long shot, but given Holly's complicated dating situation, maybe there was some sort of connection.

"No way." Brian shook his head firmly. "She was working or she was with me."

Brian's view of his mother was undoubtedly biased. From listening to how he spoke about her, it was clear he put his mother up on a pedestal, constructing an infallible portrait of a mother and woman who very likely only existed in his heart and mind. Still, his insistence that Juanita hadn't been dating anyone at the time lined up with what Ernestine had told her. That Juanita had loved her husband until the day she died despite the divorce.

They watched Brian head for a red Toyota Corolla.

"What do you think?" Simone asked Lance when they were back in the car.

"I don't know. Memories can be notoriously unreliable and he was just a kid."

"I keep thinking about the phone call Brian said his mother received the night of her murder."

"Yeah, that was new." Lance turned the car onto the street and headed back toward the center of town.

"Brian said she squealed in happiness. Given that she'd lost her job, do you think the call could have been about a new one?"

His brow furrowed. "That whoever was on the other end of the call offered her a job? I suppose it's possible."

"I think we should go see Harry Wright. One thing that seems out of character to me is the allegation of stealing made against Juanita. Nothing in her background suggests she'd have stolen from her employer. She'd worked at the pharmacy for years and no one has indicated she was in any kind of financial distress, so what made Harry accuse her and fire her for stealing?"

Lance looked thoughtful. "That's a question. I'm not sure how the answer would be helpful."

"Me either," she conceded. "But that's what chasing a story is like. Questions pop up and I chase down their answers and see where they lead me."

"Well, police work is more logical. I need to get back to the station and comb through the evidence again. And find a moment to go over to Holly Moyer's apartment again now that I know she was seeing at least one man and maybe more. I need a name for this secret boyfriend."

"Okay, then I can head to the pharmacy by myself."

Lance shot a look across the car. "No way. I thought we agreed you wouldn't go snooping around alone."

"Ah, no, we agreed I'd stay at the B and B and that we'd work together. I know you're worried, but I have to be able to do my job." She slid him a narrow-eyed stare, but he wasn't looking at her.

Tension fell off him in waves. He glanced in the rearview mirror and the SUV sped up.

"What's going on?"

"I think we are being followed," he said. "There's a black Escalade that has been behind us since we left the auto body shop."

"Is it Brian?" She turned in her seat to look out the rear window. She saw the Escalade, but she couldn't get a good look at the driver.

"Maybe. He looked to have been headed for a red Corolla, but there were plenty of cars there. He could have taken another one to throw us off his track."

The Escalade raced forward and hit the back of the SUV. The bump jerked Simone forward. She let out a scared yelp. She used her hands to brace herself against the dashboard.

Lance floored it, but the Escalade stayed on their tail.

"Press the red button on the inboard dash," he said.

She reached for it, but another bump to the rear of

the SUV sent her jerking forward again before the seat belt slammed her back against the seat.

"Are you okay?" Lance barked.

Her chest hurt where the belt had restrained her, but considering the circumstances she said, "Yes. Fine."

She reached for the button again, connecting the call this time.

A woman answered. "Carling Lake Sheriff's Department."

"This is Sheriff Webb. A black Escalade is trying to force me off the road. I'm on Route 7 headed west toward downtown. I've got a civilian, Simone Jarrett, in the car with me. I need assistance immediately."

"Got it, Sheriff. Dispatching units now. Stay on the line."

The SUV bounced along the road. Thankfully traffic was very light. Lance hit the switch to turn on the sirens, which sent the cars in front of them moving over out of the lane. Unfortunately, the sirens and lights had not dissuaded their pursuer.

"Sheriff, backup is seven minutes out."

Simone's breath hitched. Seven minutes may as well be seventy. It felt like a lifetime at the moment.

Lance pressed down hard on the gas pedal. The SUV shot forward. So did the Escalade. They were nearing a blind curve up ahead. If there was a vehicle in the lane in front of them, there was no way they'd avoid a collision.

The road began to curve.

Simone held her breath.

The asphalt stretched out before them, barren of traffic.

Behind them the Escalade sped up, ramming into the back of the SUV with enough force to send them into a spin.

"Hang on!" Lance yanked on the wheel, righting the vehicle.

The Escalade rammed them again, harder this time, sending the SUV into another tailspin. Lance cranked the wheel, sending them shooting across two lanes, over the shoulder and into the tall grass that ran parallel to the highway in a hail of squealing tires, dirt and gravel before they came to a stop.

For a long moment, Simone didn't move. Didn't so much as breathe. Then she turned, wanting to see where the Escalade was. Was it still after them?

But the Escalade was nowhere to be seen.

"Are you okay?" Lance asked.

She swallowed and took stock. Adrenaline pumped through her veins along with fear. She'd probably have a bruise on her chest from the seat belt and she was shaking. "I think so."

"Sheriff, are you still with me?" The dispatcher's voice filled the car.

"We're still here. Whoever it was ran us off the road. I'll need a tow truck. And have patrol be on the lookout for a black Escalade with probable front-end damage."

Simone doubted the sheriff's deputies would find the Escalade, at least not with the driver inside. Anyone who had the gall to try to run a sheriff's SUV off the road would know to have a plan for getting away.

"Do you think it was Brian Byers?" she asked Lance.

The look in his eyes was fierce. "I don't know, but you can bet I plan to find out."

Chapter Seventeen

Once he was sure the Escalade was gone, Lance jumped out of the car and hurried around it. Simone already had her door open and she got out, falling to her knees beside it.

He knelt beside her and gathered her in his arms. She clung to him, shaking. It was just the adrenaline rush, he knew, but that knowledge didn't stop the fear that coursed through him.

His heart beat wildly. "Here, let me help you."

Simone opened her mouth, but no sound came out. Her face blanched.

He wanted to keep her in his arms, to stay as close to her as possible, but he forced himself to pull away from the embrace just enough to run his eyes over her. She didn't look to be injured, but her eyes were unfocused and she was trembling. He was afraid she was going into shock.

He reached for his phone.

"I need an ambulance," he said when the dispatcher picked up this time. "I've got a woman who might be in shock."

Lance wrapped an arm around Simone's waist and helped her to her feet. She leaned against him and he opened the back hatch so she could sit on the ledge of the trunk.

A few minutes later they were joined by Deputy Bridges and an ambulance. Two other deputies directed traffic around the scene. So far they hadn't had a sighting of the Escalade. It seemed to have simply disappeared.

They moved into the back of the ambulance so the EMTs could check on Simone while Bridges took both of their statements.

"Did either of you happen to get a look at the plates?"

Lance shook his head.

Simone closed her eyes, seemingly to pull up the image of the Escalade right before it hit them the first time. "There were no plates." She had a focused look on her face. "The windshield was tinted. I couldn't see the driver clearly, but I think it was a man."

"Sorry to interrupt, but we should get moving to the hospital." The EMT pulled a pressure cuff from Simone's arm.

"I don't need to go to the hospital."

The EMT grabbed a clipboard from the seat next to him. "You'll have to sign this, then."

Lance frowned as he watched her sign the paper declining transportation to the hospital. "Simone. I think you should reconsider."

She was looking much better than she had when

they first got out of the car, but he wanted to be sure she wasn't injured.

Simone handed the clipboard back to the EMT and got to her feet. "I'm fine, Lance. It was just the initial adrenaline dump. This person forcing us off the road, the threat in my apartment, it just means we're on the right track."

"It also means someone is feeling very threatened and that makes them dangerous."

Simone glared at him. "I'm not backing away. We still have time to get to Wright's Pharmacy. I'm going with or without you."

Lance grumbled deep in his throat. "Deputy Bridges, I'm going to take your vehicle. Can you deal with getting mine towed and get a ride back to the station?"

The deputy saluted. "No problem, Sheriff."

They made the drive to Wright's Pharmacy in silence, both stewing in a combination of anger and fear resulting from the brazen highway attack.

The bell on the door jingled as they entered. The establishment was named Wright's Pharmacy, but in addition to filling household prescriptions, the store sold various sundry items like toothpaste, diapers and an assortment of snacks and candies. It wasn't a large space, about the size of the Pick and Go at the gas station, which allowed the entire space to be seen from the slightly elevated checkout counter. A photo of Harry Wright, his late wife, Tracey, and a young woman who Lance recognized as Harry's daughter from her infrequent visits to town over the years was perched on the shelf behind Wright's head. They all wore smocks with Wright's Pharmacy stitched over the breast pocket.

Wright was behind the counter. A short, fat man with a plethora of curly gray hair still adorning his head, he wore round wire-rimmed glasses, a white smock and a smile Lance had always felt teetered on the brink of smarmy. Small-town life all but demanded the residents patronize local businesses, so he made sure to pop into Wright's regularly, but he just didn't trust Wright with his prescriptions. Those he had sent to the chain pharmacy just outside of town.

"Good evening, Sheriff. How may I help you today?"

"Evening, Harry. I don't know if you've met Simone Jarrett. She's a reporter for the *Weekly*."

Wright focused his smile on Simone. "I've heard about the new hotshot reporter Aaron was able to recruit to our little slice of heaven but can't say I've had the pleasure of a formal introduction." Wright stretched his hand across the counter. "Harry Wright. It's a pleasure to meet you."

Simone placed her hand in his and smiled gamely. "Nice to meet you."

The handshake went on for a little too long for Lance's taste. And he didn't love the appraising look Wright swept over Simone as they shook. Part of it was pure jealousy; he doubted he'd have liked any man touching Simone even for something as benign as a handshake. And part of it was his general dislike of Wright. But whatever the cause, he was a second shy of wrenching Wright's hand away when Simone pulled her hand back.

"Harry, I've got a few questions for you. About Juanita Byers."

Harry's eyes widened in surprise. "Juanita. I haven't heard her name in years."

"Yes, well, you've probably heard about the woman we found out by Watercress and that there may be a connection between this most recent murder and Juanita's."

"I saw the story in the *Weekly*," Wright said. "Yours, I guess?" He nodded at Simone. "You really think the Card Killer is back, Sheriff?"

"I'm investigating every angle. Can you tell me about Juanita?"

Harry rubbed his chin. "Oh, well, she was a good woman. Hard worker. Good mother. All she ever talked about was her boy. I was really sad to hear what happened to her."

"Mr. Wright—" Simone started.

"Please, call me Harry."

Simone returned his smile. "Harry, I've spoken with Juanita's family and they say that you let her go just before she was murdered."

Wright busied himself arranging the display of lip balm on the counter. "You can't possibly think that had anything to do with what happened to poor Juanita."

"As I said, I'm investigating all possibilities," Lance said.

"Well, I did have to let her go not long before…

you know." Wright stopped fussing with the display and sighed. "She'd always been a good worker. Reliable. Dependable. Trustworthy."

The woman the pharmacist was describing did not sound like a thief. "Juanita's sister said you fired her for stealing," Lance said.

Wright nodded. "I had to. A hundred and twenty-seven dollars was missing from the register. Funny how I still remember the exact amount."

"And despite how good a worker, how trustworthy you'd always found Juanita to be, you thought she took the money?" Lance pressed.

Wright's eyes fell to the counter. He picked at his cuticle. "I did."

The antenna on Lance's internal lie detector went up.

Simone spoke first. "Did? Do you still think Juanita stole the money?"

Wright kept looking at the counter. "Of course I do. Who else could it have been?" he said without conviction.

He was lying. And not well.

Lance's gaze fell to the photo on the shelf behind the older man's head. A suspicion niggled at him.

"Did your daughter work here at the same time as Juanita?"

Wright's body jerked. "Sarah? She never…she never worked here. Where did you get that idea?"

Lance pointed to the photo of Harry's family that he'd noticed when he entered the pharmacy. "It looks like she did."

Wright turned to look where Lance pointed. His face was red when he turned back to them. "She helped out from time to time."

"During the time Juanita worked for you?" Simone asked.

Wright pressed his lips together in a tight line.

"It won't be that hard to get an answer to that question. There'll be records. People who remember seeing Sarah and Juanita here at the same time," Simone said.

Wright shot a glare her way.

Lance took a step forward, drawing Wright's attention from Simone. "If I need to, I can go talk to Sarah, but I don't think you want me to do that."

Wright visibly deflated. "No. No, you don't have to do that. Juanita didn't steal the money. Sarah did. She'd developed a drug problem. I didn't know that at the time," he added quickly. "I would have never fired Juanita if I'd thought Sarah had stolen the money."

"But when you found out, you didn't give Juanita her job back," Simone pointed out.

Harry crossed his arms over his chest. "I didn't find out Sarah had stolen the money until after I'd fired Juanita. I was struggling with what to do about it. I couldn't just rehire Juanita after accusing her of theft, but I felt bad. She had a kid to support. But before I could figure it out, Juanita was killed."

Lance frowned. "Yet, you still didn't tell the truth."

"It didn't seem like there was any point. Juanita was gone. Telling the truth wasn't going to bring her back. And if I told the truth, I'd ruin Sarah's reputation."

"So you just let Juanita's reputation be sullied for the last twenty years," Simone said, disgust clear in her tone.

"Look, I'm not proud of what I did, but I'd do it again. Sarah was in bad shape by the time I realized what was going on. It took everything my wife and I had to convince her to go into rehab. We kept it quiet, telling people she'd gone overseas to study for a semester, so that when she got back to town, no one would look at her any differently."

Lance wasn't buying it, which Harry must have seen.

"Neither of you has children," he said. "If you did, you'd understand. You'd have done the same."

There was no way Lance would have let a murder victim's reputation be sullied by a lie for twenty years, but arguing with Harry wasn't the best use of his time at the moment. "Is there anything else from that time that you haven't told me?"

Harry paused. "I remember hearing that Juanita might have found a job."

"When was this?" Lance said.

"Right around the time she was murdered. I heard that she'd interviewed with the paper."

"The *Carling Lake Weekly*?" Simone said with surprise.

Harry nodded. "Yes. I contemplated calling Aaron and putting in a good word, but I wasn't sure how to do it without arousing his suspicions. I mean, I'd just fired her for theft. But before I could decide what to do, she was killed."

"Okay, Wright." Lance tapped the counter. "If you think of anything else, give me a call."

Lance and Simone stepped out onto the sidewalk.

"I'm not sure how to feel about Harry Wright," Simone said.

He understood the feeling. He couldn't condone the man's decisions all those years ago, but parents often did all manner of questionable things when it came to their kids. They only needed to look at the college admissions scandal for proof of that.

"I need to talk to Aaron," Lance said. He looked at his watch. It was after seven.

Simone's face scrounged in thought. "Me too. I want to ask him why he never mentioned Juanita's interviewed at the *Weekly*."

He was interested in the answer to that question himself, but there were a thousand possible reasons. "We don't know that she did. Only that Harry heard that she had."

"True." Simone conceded. "I need to update him on where my story stands so I'll ask him then."

He let out a deep breath. "You can update him on your story if you need to, but I need to broach the subject of Juanita's possible employment."

"Well, let's go then. We might still be able to catch him at the *Weekly*'s offices."

But the office was empty and dark when they got there. Simone tried Aaron's cell but got no answer.

"You want to take a drive out to his house?" Simone asked.

He ran a hand over his head. The truth about the theft that led to Juanita's firing and her possible new job with the *Weekly* was new information but it didn't really move his case forward even if it turned out to be true. The theft nor the new job were a motive for murder. "No. It can wait until tomorrow. Why don't I drive you to the B and B?"

She shook her head. "You don't have to do that. I need to pick up my car from my apartment anyway to get into town tomorrow."

He put a hand on her back and led her to the car. "I'll give you a lift into town tomorrow. I don't want you going anywhere alone."

He held the door open for her to hop into the passenger side of the SUV.

She rolled her eyes and drew her legs into the car. "Don't you think you're being a bit overprotective?"

He shot her a smile and closed the door before he answered in a soft voice, "Not at all."

He pulled into a parking space in the B and B's lot not long after they left the newspaper's offices.

He grabbed the bag he'd packed earlier that morning from the back seat of the SUV and walked with Simone through the front doors.

Erika stood at the semicircular reception desk in the foyer next to the stairs leading to the second floor of the house where the guest rooms were. Off to the left of the foyer was the large eat-in kitchen. To the right was the parlor, which Erika had turned into a relaxing gathering space for her guests.

"Thanks for seeing me to the door," Simone said, turning to him at the bottom of the stairs.

"Not a problem." He turned to Erika. "Checking in."

Both women looked at him with surprise written on their faces.

"What are you doing?" Simone asked.

"Checking in. I think you'll see that I have a reservation for the next two nights, although I was assured that if I need to extend my stay, that would be accommodated." He pointed to the computer on the desk.

Erika tapped a few keys. "He does have a reservation, but I didn't make it."

"I did." James West strode from the kitchen. "Lance called earlier today saying he needed a room. Of course, I made it happen."

Erika narrowed her eyes at her husband. "Of course you did."

Lance was ready when Simone whirled on him. "You don't need a room."

"And how would you know that?"

She fisted her hands on her hips. "You invited me to stay in your guest room. Why would you do that if there was a problem with your house?"

"I didn't know there was a problem until I got home this morning. Found a few creepy crawlers. Decided to have the entire place fumigated."

She shook her head. "This was not our deal."

"Our deal didn't say anything about me staying at the B and B."

She threw up her hands. "Fine. Whatever. I'm going to my room." She stomped up the stairs and disappeared on the second-floor landing.

James shook his head. "I told you this wouldn't go over well."

Lance leaned against the reception desk, shooting his friend a small smile. "It actually went better than I thought it would."

He wasn't surprised to find Simone waiting for him when he got to the second floor. She stood in the doorway of what he assumed was her room.

James had placed him in the room right next to hers.

"You know, I'm not some helpless woman in need of a man to watch over her and protect her."

"I never said you were."

"But you're acting like it."

Exhausted and still shaken from being driven off the road, an event that could have seriously hurt him or her, his last thread of finesse snapped.

He dropped his bag on the floor outside her door and stepped in close until there were only centimeters between the two of them. "I'm acting like a man who cares about you."

Simone jerked as if the words had physically assaulted her.

They stared at each other for a long torturous moment before he stepped back.

"I'm in the room next door if you need me." He picked his bag up off the floor. "Good night, Simone." She closed her door without another word.

Chapter Eighteen

James was already in the kitchen when Lance came downstairs the next morning. His friend took one look at his face, grabbed a mug from the shelf above the counter and poured into it from the coffeepot in front of him.

"You look like you need this." James slid the black coffee across the counter to Lance.

"Thank you. I do."

Lance took a long swig.

"So. You and Simone, huh?" James grinned over the rim of his cup.

"I guess the whole town knows, then?"

"I don't know about the whole town. I didn't suspect anything until Erika clued me in and I'm a trained investigator supposedly, so I'd say you guys have been doing well hiding your relationship. I do wonder *why* you're hiding your relationship." James took another sip.

"I'm starting to wonder myself. At first, it made sense. Neither of us wanted to get into anything serious."

"But now?"

"I'm serious." Lance took another big sip while the import of what he'd said hit him. He was serious about Simone. Somewhere along the way, their casual relationship had turned into something real. At least for him. And he hoped for her.

James leaned against the counter and pinned him with a look. "How does Simone feel?"

"I have no idea."

"Don't you think you two should talk about it?"

"Yes, but there's so much going on right now. I mean I just found out that she might have seen the Card Killer murder his last victim twenty years ago and now it looks like she's become his target."

"And you are terrified for her and terrified that she might not want to take your relationship to the next level at the same time."

"That pretty much sums it up."

"Take it from me—it's best to get it all out there and deal with it. I almost lost Erika by keeping secrets, trying not to feel too much for her. It always backfires."

"I remember. And I get it, I do." Lance finished his coffee and set the mug aside. "I just think this is not like your situation with Erika."

"It never is. But at the core, a relationship is built on honesty and trust, so if you want a relationship with Simone, you have to come clean with her. And let her come clean with you because it's better that you know you two don't want the same thing now than to find out later."

He knew James was right, but that didn't make the idea of Simone deciding that she didn't want to take their relationship to the next level any easier to bear.

The sound of footsteps falling on the wood staircase brought his conversation with James to an end.

Simone stepped into the kitchen, dressed in jeans and a blouse, her messenger bag slung across her shoulder. She directed a small smile toward James. "Good morning, James. Lance." She didn't look his way as she said his name. He supposed it was something that she even acknowledged him, given how angry she'd been the night before.

Well, too bad. He wasn't going to apologize for caring about her. The security at the B and B was top-notch, yes, and James undoubtedly had the skills to protect her, but no one would protect her the way he would. He'd lay down his life for her if he had to.

"Erika left homemade scones for the two of you for breakfast." James gestured to the covered dish on the breakfast table. "I'm not a chef, but I can whip up an omelet if you need something more substantial."

"A scone is more than enough for me. I'm not a big breakfast eater," Simone answered.

"I'm good. Thanks, James," Lance said.

"Okay, then I'll leave you two to your day." He headed for the door at the rear of the kitchen that led to the West family's private quarters but stopped as he passed Lance. "If you need me, I'm just a phone call away."

"Thanks, man."

"What was that all about?" Simone asked after James disappeared.

"Nothing. Are you ready? I can drop you at the *Weekly* on the way into the station."

"I can drive myself." She turned her back on him and wrapped two scones in a napkin, tucking them into her purse.

He tamped down irritation. "No, you can't. You don't have your car, remember?"

She turned to face him, hissing out a breath.

"Look, I know you're angry with me. I should have told you I made a reservation at the B and B. I'm sorry. But I'm not sorry about wanting to protect you."

"I don't need protection. I was shaken up by the break-in at my apartment, but I can take care of myself."

"I know you can." He reached for her and was thrilled when she let him pull her to him. He rested his forehead against hers. "I'm just saying…" What was he saying? That her voice when she'd called about the break-in had been the single scariest sound he'd ever heard. That he was terrified of losing her. That he thought he was falling in love with her. Every one of those statements was true, but he feared that any of them might drive her away. "I'm just saying I don't want you to get hurt."

She pressed a kiss to his lips and something inside him stilled. He drew her closer.

"I appreciate that. I do. But no more of this macho, protecting the little lady stuff. You have to trust me to take care of myself and to know that I will call you if I need your help, okay?"

"Okay."

She kissed him again. "Come on. We both have work to do."

THE WHINE OF a power drill could be heard before the elevator doors opened to the *Weekly*'s offices.

Simone stepped out of the elevator with Lance by her side and took in the scene.

The drill was wielded by a dark-haired man on a ladder in the conference room. Several panels in the ceiling had been removed and wires hung like vines waiting to be climbed.

Aaron's office was empty and Margaret, the only employee of the *Weekly* who was present as far as Simone could tell, sat at her desk.

"What's going on?" Simone asked, dropping her messenger bag onto her desk across from Margaret's.

Margaret looked away from her monitor, a bit of surprise in her eyes, and that was when Simone noticed she was wearing noise-canceling headphones.

Margaret pulled the headphones from her ears, letting them rest around her neck. "Morning, Simone. Sheriff. Sorry about the noise. We've got some kind of electrical wiring issue. If you don't have earphones, you might want to work from home today."

It looked like that was exactly what Zane and Aaron were doing. Neither was in the office.

"It's fine," Simone said, forcing a smile. She shifted her gaze to Aaron's empty office. "How's the chief?"

What she really wanted to ask was had he cooled off. And if she had a better than fifty-fifty chance of keeping her job the next time she saw him.

Margaret seemed to get the hint. "He's calmed down, but you're going to be on his naughty list for a while yet. Lucky for you, he's taking a bit of time off. Wrenched his back last evening, so he's taking it easy today."

Lance tapped his hand against his thigh. "That might be lucky for Simone, but not for me."

Margaret gave him a look of surprise. "Oh? Why?"

"I wanted to talk to him about someone. An old employee of the *Weekly*."

Margaret smiled. "Well, I'm sure I can help you with that, Sheriff Webb. Most people think of me as the part-time reporter, but technically I'm also co-owner of the paper. I do try to keep up with the business side, although that is more Aaron's bailiwick. I'll give it a go for you though."

"Okay, then. A couple of questions have come up in the course of my current investigation," Lance said.

Margaret's brow lifted. "Which one? By my count, you've got four unsolved murders on your hands."

"Yes, well, it looks more and more like they are all connected. Simone and I spoke with Harry Wright yesterday," Lance said. "I don't know if you remember, but Juanita Byers worked for him before she was killed."

Margaret leaned back in her ergonomic chair. "I think I do recall that."

"Harry let Juanita go a few weeks before her death. For stealing," Simone continued.

"As it turns out, he was wrong about that. She wasn't the person who stole from him," Lance said with a touch of disdain in his tone.

"Right, right. It's all coming back to me now." Margaret leaned forward and folded her hands on her desk. "I'm not surprised Harry was wrong about Juanita. She was a fine woman as I remember. Not the type of person to steal. Not even if she was down to her last dime. She just didn't have a criminal bone in her body." Margaret shook her head, a sad expression on her face.

"Wright said he thought Juanita interviewed for a job with the *Weekly* after he fired her. I'm wondering if you can confirm that," Lance said.

Margaret nodded. "I can. That's to say he would have offered her a job. We decided to hire an assistant. It just got to be overwhelming. Juanita interviewed. Aaron and I didn't believe the gossip about her stealing. I had a good feeling about her, and frankly, we needed the help. We agreed to give Juanita the job, but she was killed before Aaron made the offer."

Simone felt a wave of sadness wash over her. Juanita had been so close to getting her life back on track and then someone had just stolen it away from her.

"So Juanita never knew she'd gotten the job?" Lance said.

Margaret shook her head forlornly. "No."

"Thanks, Margaret." Lance backed away from Margaret's desk.

Simone followed. They didn't have to go far for privacy, since the work in the conference room masked their conversation.

"Well, there goes our theory that the call Juanita got the night of her murder was about a job."

"Not exactly. It could have been about a job we don't know about yet. And I still want to talk to Aaron."

Simone's eyes moved to her boss's empty office. "Me too. Can you give me a minute, please? I need to talk to Margaret."

"Sure." Lance walked away to the elevators.

"Margaret, I've already apologized to Aaron, but I want to apologize to you too. I know that withholding those pictures and not telling you and Aaron about my connection to the Card Killer cases was unprofessional and wrong. I just wanted to let you know that it won't happen again."

Margaret frowned. "Aaron was livid. I have to tell you he was this close to firing you." She held her thumb and forefinger a millimeter apart.

"Margaret—"

She held up her hand. "I'm not going to say I condone what you did. I don't. But I understand it, I think." Her eyes darkened and fixed on Simone's like lasers. "But if you ever lie to either of us or hold back on a story again, that's it for you at the *Weekly*. Do we understand each other?"

"Perfectly." She gave Margaret a weak smile. That was the best she could have hoped for and she was glad the apology tour was over. Now she just had to earn back the trust of her employers. She had a lot of work ahead of her to repair the relationship with her boss, but she felt like there was a path there, so that was something.

She caught up with Lance waiting by the elevators.

He held his phone to his ear and raised a finger when she stopped by his side. From the expression on his face, he didn't like whatever the person on the other end of the call was saying.

She waited for him to end the call, then asked, "What was that all about?"

"No sign of the Escalade. This is one time I wish Carling Lake was more like the big cities with cameras on every corner."

"You'll find it. An Escalade is a pretty big car to hide forever. Eventually, the driver will take it to a body shop to get fixed."

"Let's hope it's one close by. I'm having my deputies put out a BOLO to every automotive shop within fifty miles, but if the driver does the work himself, or goes farther out, or pays someone enough to look the other way, that may be a dead end." His lips pinched together.

She resisted the urge to sweep her fingers over his cheek and kiss away his frustration. "I'm going to stay here and get some work done."

"You sure?"

"Yes, I'm sure. I need to catch up with my intern. She hasn't returned my texts or calls."

"Be careful. Don't leave the office by yourself. I'll call to check in on you later."

Simone rolled her eyes. "You mean check up on me."

"Potato. Potahto." Lance leaned in slightly, then caught himself, jerking backward.

Simone glanced over her shoulder, but Margaret had her back to them, her headphones back in place. Simone brushed a kiss over Lance's lips, feeling like a teenager stealing a kiss with her boyfriend.

Lance grinned. "See you later."

The elevator doors slid open and a moment later he was gone.

Now, where was Kate? Obviously not in the office. The entirety of the *Carling Lake Weekly*'s domain could be seen from where Simone stood.

Annoyance welled inside her. She dialed Kate's number. The phone rang several times before Kate's voice mail kicked in.

"Hey, where are you? Call me when you get this."

Something was wrong. They hadn't worked together long, but Kate had the makings of a good reporter. She was smart, fast and hungry for the story. She wouldn't just blow off work or phone calls.

She went back to Margaret's desk. "Margaret, have you talked to Kate today?" she yelled over the noise from the conference room.

Margaret looked up, pulling her headphones off again. Simone repeated the question. "No, actually, and she's usually in by now."

"I know. She didn't answer my call either. I'm going to walk over to her place. Make sure everything is okay."

Margaret gave her a thumbs-up, replaced her headphones over her ears and went back to whatever was on her computer screen.

Simone grabbed her messenger bag and headed for the elevators. Kate had rented a small place a block from the *Weekly*'s offices for the semester. It was a bit of a drive from Carling Lake to Stunnersville on the two days she had class, but she'd been excited to be out of the dorms and on her own.

The apartment was on the top floor of a four-level walk-up. The front door to the building was unlocked, so Simone bounded up the steps to Kate's apartment.

She knocked on the door. "Kate? It's Simone. Are you there?"

The sound of glass breaking came from the other side of the door.

"Kate?" She knocked again, tension coiling in her body.

A thump sounded as if something heavy had fallen.

She turned the doorknob, finding it unlocked. "I'm coming in."

She took a split second to process what she was seeing. An end table was turned on its side, a shattered drinking glass beside it, and the couch cushions were strewn on the living room floor.

Kate lay on the floor in front of the sofa, angry red welts blooming on her neck around a thin piece of flexible wire.

Simone rushed to her side, unwrapping the wire from Kate's neck as quickly and gently as she could. She pressed two fingers against the side of Kate's neck, her hand shaking so violently she wasn't sure she'd be able to find a pulse even if one was there.

"Please. Please. Please."

There. It was faint, but there was a pulse.

She dug her phone out of her bag and dialed 911, giving the operator Kate's address.

"Hang on, Kate. Hang on."

She knelt next to Kate, taking her hand as she listened to the operator's assurances that help was on the way. A piece of paper she hadn't noticed earlier crinkled under her knees.

She recognized it as a page from the incident report for Juanita Byers's murder.

Sandwiching her phone between her chin and ear, she took a good look around.

The papers from the file she'd given Kate on the Card Killer's murders lay scattered over the carpeted floor. She must have had them on the overturned table.

Sirens sounded through the open apartment door. EMTs followed moments later.

Simone stood aside to let them work, wrapping her arms around her midsection to stave off the chill that was sweeping through her body.

This was no random attack.

The killer had come after Kate.

Chapter Nineteen

Worry wouldn't let Simone sit, so she paced the waiting room. She'd given a brief description of what happened to the responding deputy, then rode to the hospital with Kate in the ambulance, but she'd only been allowed to go as far as the ER waiting room. Even in the early evening, it was crowded. She'd found a second waiting area at the far end of the hall, this one blessedly deserted, and left word with the triage nurse where she could be found.

The quiet brought its own difficulties.

Her mind kept flashing back to Kate's pale, lifeless face and weak pulse.

Simone carried the watery vending machine coffee to the narrow window overlooking a small surface parking lot and wondered for the thousandth time whether her zest to find a killer was the reason Kate currently fought for her life.

She turned at the sound of heels tapping against the polished hospital floors.

Margaret swept into the waiting room. "There you are! Has there been any news?"

"The doctors haven't told me anything. They let me ride in the ambulance with her. She didn't regain consciousness on the way to the hospital."

Simone struggled against tears, unsure how she would be able to put herself back together if she broke. She just needed to know Kate would be okay.

Margaret reached for her hand, squeezing it. "I'm sure she'll be okay." It was a sympathetic gesture that had the effect of putting Simone even more on edge.

"I've called her parents," Margaret said, leading Simone back to the row of hard plastic chairs. "They're driving up from Pennsylvania. What happened?"

Simone swallowed hard. "I knocked and then there was a crash and a sound like someone had fallen." She flashed back to opening Kate's apartment door and the horror of seeing her lying motionless on the floor. "I tried the knob and the door was unlocked, so I went in. She was on the floor. Margaret, someone tried to strangle her."

Margaret's eyes widened in shock and understanding.

"Simone?" She looked away from Margaret's stunned gaze to see Lance marching through the waiting room doors.

She hadn't called him, but of course word of a possible strangulation would make it to the sheriff.

Simone shot to her feet and moved toward him, the slight shake of his head stopping her from launching herself into his arms.

"Has there been any word on Ms. Morelli's condition?" Lance asked, stopping a respectable distance in front of Simone, his light brown eyes locked on hers.

Margaret stood up and made her way to them, completing the trio, her curious gaze darting between Simone and Lance.

"Nothing yet." Tension laced Simone's voice, not all of it due to her fear and worry over Kate's prognosis.

Every fiber in her body wanted to lean into Lance, to absorb his strength for just a moment. Not so long ago she would have seen the inclination to do so as a weakness. But somehow over the last several months since they'd been together, she'd come to realize that it wasn't a weakness to depend upon someone else sometimes. She was no less the kick-ass, self-sufficient woman she'd been before giving in to her attraction to Lance. Knowing he was on her side had, in an inexplicable way, made her feel stronger. It was a thought she tucked away for contemplation later.

Lance focused on Simone again. "I need to get the details of what happened from you, Simone."

Margaret backed away. "I'll see if I can get an update on Kate while you two talk."

Lance led her across the hall to a smaller room, its door marked with a consultation room sign. He held the door open so she could enter. The room had a small round table and four chairs.

She turned as the door snapped closed and stepped into him, her arms slipping under his leather coat and around his back. He pulled her close, resting his chin against the top of her head. The warmth of his body enveloped her and some of the fear and shock she'd been feeling since finding Kate dissipated.

They stood that way for several minutes, neither of them talking or moving. She felt herself settle with each passing minute and a realization hit her.

She wanted this.

This kind of closeness.

And not just with anyone.

With Lance. Only Lance.

Her body tensed with the realization. She knew that wouldn't change, just like she knew a secret relationship wasn't a relationship at all. There'd be challenges with their jobs, but what relationship didn't have its challenges? Her brain turned over the possible ways to make it work.

Lance must have felt the shift in her mood.

"You okay?" He pulled back, studying her face, his arms still locked around her waist.

"Yes. It's just…everything."

He pulled her back to him. "You have no idea how scared I was when you called."

She pressed her face into his chest. "I was never in any danger. It was Kate—"

"You don't know that. My deputy said you heard a scuffle and someone fall. The perpetrator was likely in the apartment when you arrived."

Simone stilled. She'd not thought about that at the time, but he was right. She'd been so focused on helping Kate that she'd not considered whether there was anyone else in the apartment, but there had to have been, at least when she'd first knocked. No one had come out the front door, she was sure of that.

"The window," Simone said at the same time the door to the room swung open.

"Sheriff Webb, you in here?"

Deputy Bridges's gaze swept over them. Lance's arms were still wrapped around her, their bodies far too close together for the embrace to be passed off as simple comforting.

The deputy's face flamed red. "Oh, sorry. I should have knocked." He stepped back out of the room.

Lance stepped away from her and let his arms drop to his sides. "Bridges, you can come in. Simone was just about to take me through what happened. You should hear it too."

Bridges stepped back into the room, his face still red. He shot a quick, apologetic glance Simone's way before moving to stand next to Lance. Both men pulled small notebooks and pens from their inside breast pockets.

"Simone, why don't you walk us through everything that happened leading up to finding Ms. Morelli."

Simone relayed the same story she'd told Margaret.

"It's my fault Kate was attacked." She crossed her arms over her stomach, the guilt so potent it felt as if it was trying to claw its way out of her. "With the threat and the break-in at my place, I should have done something to protect her. Take her off the story. I just didn't think."

Lance reached out and ran a hand down her arm.

"Simone, it doesn't do any good to blame yourself. The only person to blame is the person who attacked Kate. Do you know if she received the same type of threats you did?"

"I don't think so. She never mentioned it," Simone answered. She didn't think Kate would have kept it from her if she'd received a threat.

"It's possible the person who attacked Ms. Morelli isn't the same guy who killed Holly Moyer," Deputy Bridges offered. "I had a quick look at Ms. Morelli's apartment and we didn't find a playing card like we did at the other scene."

Simone shook her head. She knew in her gut Kate had been attacked by the killer because she'd been working on the story with Simone. "I interrupted him. He didn't have time to leave his calling card."

"Why don't you head back to the apartment," Lance said to Bridges. "See if there's anything else you can find."

She thought back to walking into Kate's apartment. Had she seen any part of the attacker? Anything that would help Lance identify and stop this madman? But she couldn't produce even a shadow. She'd been solely focused on Kate's lifeless body.

"Wait," Simone ordered.

Bridges stopped with the door partially open.

"Look for a bracelet. I gave Kate a bracelet with a flash drive inside. It had all my files on the Card Killer on it. It wasn't on her wrist when I found her."

A brisk knock sounded and Margaret's head peeked around the door. "The doctor came by with an update on Kate's condition. They're concerned about the loss of oxygen to her brain. She's in a medically induced coma. They'll know more in twenty-four hours."

"So now what?" Helplessness threatened to overwhelm her.

No one answered because the answer was clear. They waited to see if Kate survived.

Margaret squeezed into the small room. Wrapping Simone in a hug, she said, "I'm going to go home and check on Aaron. I called to tell him the news so he wouldn't hear it from anyone else. He's very upset. You should go home when you leave here."

She squeezed Margaret before letting her go. She wasn't sure what she was going to do, but going back to the B and B didn't seem like the right answer. More than ever, she wanted to find the answers that led to the identity of the Card Killer.

Margaret left, shutting the door behind her just as Lance's phone beeped.

"Nancy Oliver's father returned my call. He's willing to speak with me today," he said.

Simone's chest tightened and another wave of guilt flooded her body. Another person whose life she'd had a hand in destroying.

"You don't have to come with me," Lance said quietly.

A large part of her wanted to run just like she'd done all those years ago. Let Lance talk to Nancy's father. It was his job. But a bigger part of her wanted to stop the animal who had roamed Carling Lake's streets with impunity for far too long. Maybe what she was seeking now was something closer to revenge than justice, but she didn't care.

She'd come back to Carling Lake to do what was right and catch a killer and she was more motivated than ever.

"No, I'm going with you," she said, looking into his eyes. "I've come this far. I'm not about to stop now."

Chapter Twenty

Lance processed Kate's apartment and sent what scant evidence they had to be analyzed while Bridges interviewed Kate's neighbors. Most had been at work. No one had seen or heard anything helpful. But it didn't appear that the assailant had broken in, which likely meant Kate had let him in. This was in keeping with the Card Killer's ability to put his victims at ease. Attacking Kate in her apartment, where any number of neighbors could have been home and seen or heard something, however, was out of character.

And that scared him.

Attacking Kate smacked of desperation and a desperate killer was a more dangerous killer. He had to find the killer and put him in a cage. Now.

He glanced at Simone sitting in the passenger seat of the police cruiser. The sun was making its final descent over the mountains and its last rays of the day shimmered in the highlights of her hair. She'd spent most of the day at the hospital, but when he'd told her that Nancy Oliver's father had finally returned his call, she'd insisted on making the trip with him to talk to the man.

Lance parked in front of a redbrick ranch-style home with a tidy and well-cared-for yard. A gold sedan was parked in the driveway behind a teardrop camper.

They walked up the concrete walkway and rang the doorbell.

The sound of a television came from inside the house and footsteps grew louder. Moments later the door opened and a man with long gray hair pulled back in a ponytail and sad green eyes stared out at them.

"Sheriff Webb?" the man asked.

"Yes." Lance offered his hand. "This is Simone Jarrett. She's a reporter with the *Carling Lake Weekly.*"

"Wendell Oliver." Oliver gave Lance's hand a perfunctory shake and frowned. "I didn't agree to talk to any reporters."

"And if you'd prefer, I'll wait in the car while you and the sheriff speak," Simone said. "But I'm working on a story about the women believed to have been killed by the Card Killer in hopes that there's someone out there who knows something and is willing to share it now. Knowing more about Nancy and the other women might help to bring their killer to justice."

The man stared for a beat.

"Nancy and the other women have been gone for twenty years. I doubt anyone is going to show up pointing the finger now."

"Isn't it worth a try? Isn't that why you agreed to talk to Sheriff Webb?"

The man hesitated for a moment longer, then pushed the door open wider. "Come on in."

They entered the dimly lit house. The air conditioner must have been turned to the highest possible setting. Stepping into the house felt like stepping into the Antarctic. Lance saw Simone shiver.

A crucifix hung on the wall over the dark green sectional sofa. On the opposite wall, a television held the space of honor, flanked by two large glass display cases on either side filled with sports memorabilia. There were a couple of signed baseballs, and several autographed photos of players from MLB, the NBA and the NHL. Even a signed Barry Sanders rookie card. Mr. Oliver was clearly a huge sports fan. They were looking at thousands of dollars decorating his living room.

They followed him to the sofa.

"You've got quite a collection of sports memorabilia there." Simone gestured to the shelves.

Oliver glanced at the shelves as if he'd never seen them before. "Nancy loved sports. It was the one thing we had in common." His eyes took on an even sadder sheen. "I keep thinking about selling it online. At this point in my life, the money is more important than the memories, but I haven't gotten around to it yet."

Somehow Lance doubted that Mr. Oliver would ever get rid of his collection. It was too tied to his feelings for his daughter. It had been twenty years since Nancy's murder, but the shroud of grief still hung over Wendell Oliver and his entire house.

"I'm sorry for your loss, Mr. Oliver," Lance said.

The older man turned away, but not before Lance caught the shimmer of tears in his eyes. He gave him a moment to collect himself.

"Mr. Oliver, what can you tell me about the last time you saw your daughter?"

"She was going out. She was always going out. I tried to raise her right, but after her mother passed, Nancy pulled away. Became a party girl. Started hanging with the wrong people, you know. Drinking. Smoking. She was even arrested a couple of times."

He'd seen Nancy's arrest record. Several pops for public drunkenness. One for assault after a bar fight.

"She wanted to be a dancer, so she got a job in Stunnersville," Oliver continued. "Told me it was with a dance company, but I found out later it was at one of those strip clubs in the seedy part of town. The Palace Theater."

Oliver's face reddened. "I went down there fully intending to pull her out of there. I honestly don't know what I was thinking. What if she'd been onstage when I got there?" He shuddered. "But there was some other man's daughter up there. I found Nancy in the back. I made a scene. I was determined to save my daughter that night."

"What did Nancy do?" Simone asked.

"She said I was embarrassing her. She was an adult and she'd do what she wanted. Then she had security throw me out. When I got home from work the next day, she'd moved all her stuff out."

"But she was living here at the time she was killed?" Simone queried.

Oliver shook his head. "She lost the dancing job and I offered to let her move back in but she said she was too old to live with her father. She'd been staying with a friend. I can't say I minded her losing the job, but it seemed to be a turning point. Her drinking and partying just went out of control after that."

"Did she ever mention anyone bothering her? Maybe someone from the club?"

"The sheriff back then asked me all these questions. She never mentioned anyone. We weren't talking to each other by then."

"Was she dating anyone?" Simone asked.

He scoffed. "She had a different guy every day of the week, it seemed like. I told her she should find herself a nice guy and settle down, but she always said that was the last thing she wanted to do."

"So she wasn't seeing anyone in particular that you know of?" Lance pressed.

Oliver shook his head and then stopped. "Actually, there was one guy. He came to pick her up more than once after Nancy thought I'd gone to bed. I know it was the same guy because of the car. Steel blue Mustang."

"Do you know who the guy was?" Simone asked.

"No. I think I asked once, but she wouldn't tell me his name."

Lance felt his frustration rising. They weren't getting much from Mr. Oliver. "What about a description?"

"Never saw the guy. Just the car. But Clare might know."

"Clare?"

"Clare Davenport. She and Nancy were close."

The name tickled his memory. He'd read Clare's interview, but she hadn't mentioned a boyfriend. He'd have to track her down and talk to her again.

Oliver spoke about his daughter for another twenty minutes. About the girl she'd been before her mother died. He wanted to share the hopes and dreams she'd had and that he'd had for her. Before leaving, Lance gave the man his card and said to call if he remembered anything else.

Once they were outside, he noticed Simone's hands shaking.

"Hey, are you okay?" he asked, taking her hands in his own.

"I don't know. Mr. Oliver, he seemed so broken."

"Losing a child is hard."

"If I'd told someone what I saw twenty years ago, or even ten years ago—"

He squeezed her fingers. "You can't think that way. You had to make an impossible choice for a child. Your fear was, is, understandable."

"Lance, we have to find this guy."

"We will. I promise. For now, why don't I take you back to the B and B? You can work from there for the rest of the day."

Lance pulled to a stop in front of the B and B several minutes later just as the front door opened and Erika and James stepped out onto the porch.

"I'm glad we caught you guys before we left." Erika approached the car as Simone and Lance got out. "James and I are going out for the evening, but I left a roast warming in the Crock-Pot for you two."

"I thought this was a bed-and-breakfast," Lance said. "You didn't have to make us dinner."

Erika waved a hand absently. "It was no trouble. You two are more family than guests anyway."

"A roast sounds great. I didn't realize how hungry I am until you mentioned food," Simone said.

"Babe, we're going to be late if we don't get a move on," James called from where he stood next to his sleek black SUV.

"Got to go." Erika leaned into Simone for a quick hug and said in a voice loud enough for Lance to hear, "We're going to be out late, so you two have the whole place to yourselves." She drew back and wiggled her eyebrows at them both before hustling to James's car.

The smell of the roast and root vegetables hit them the moment they stepped through the B and B's doors.

Erika had renovated much of the majestic older farmhouse before opening as a B and B, including the kitchen.

White cabinets, granite countertops and stainless steel appliances. A Crock-Pot sat on the counter, the roast complete with potatoes and carrots simmering inside. A bottle of red wine and two glasses waited next to it.

"Looks like Erika thought of everything," Lance

said. "It's a nice evening. What do you think about dining on the back porch?"

"Sounds good to me."

They made their plates and Lance carried them to the porch while she followed with the wine, glasses and silverware.

It was warm for late October and dusk had already fallen, revealing the first stars in the sky.

Lance pulled out his phone and a moment later a soulful, jazz-inspired ballad poured through the speakers.

Lance cut into the roast beef, his taste buds exploding at the perfect mix of spices. "This is great. Erika should consider serving dinner. Her business will explode."

"You're right. It is amazing." Simone chewed with her eyes closed, a rapturous expression on her face.

His body tightened in arousal.

Her eyes opened, catching him watching her. In an instant her gaze shifted, reflecting the desire he was feeling.

"So is this our official first date?" she asked.

He shook his head. "This is not a date."

"I didn't mean…"

"When I take you out on our first official date, I'll be in a suit. I'll take you to a nice restaurant so I can show all of Carling Lake that I'm with the most beautiful woman in the state. There'll be dancing."

"I can't dance."

He stood and pulled her up and into his arms.

"That's okay. I'll hold you close. You just have to follow."

They swayed next to the table in time to the rhythm he set.

"I'll take you home and walk you to your door."

She pulled back just enough to look him in the eyes. "Don't tell me you're going to continue being the perfect gentleman and leave me at my door with a chaste kiss on the cheek."

He chuckled. "Is that what you want me to do?"

"Absolutely not."

Her hands went around his neck and she brought her lips to his in a smoldering kiss.

He broke off the kiss and looked deep into her eyes. "I'm serious about that date."

"Lance." She looked at him with uncertainty in her eyes.

"I know we agreed to be casual and to keep our relationship to ourselves. But I don't want that. Not anymore. I want people to know that we are together. I want a real relationship."

She tensed. "I don't know."

"I get that there's a lot going on right now. I'm not asking you to decide today. Just will you think about it?"

He felt her relax in his arms. "I will think about it."

He dipped his head and nibbled on her earlobe. "Just so you know, I plan to use every tool in my considerable arsenal to convince you to take a chance on me."

She giggled. "Oh, you do, do you?"

"Absolutely. Beginning right now."

His hands went to her lower back and pulled her body tightly against his. He kissed his way up her neck and back to her lips.

Moments later, they found their way up the stairs and into Simone's room.

He fumbled blindly to close the room door without letting go of Simone. He felt her hand on his chest, a feathery, gentle touch. Their kiss deepened, the taste of her lips somehow sweeter and more sensual than he'd ever felt before. She slid his jacket off his shoulders.

His hands slid beneath her cotton shirt. They broke apart only long enough for him to rid her of it and for him to shed his own shirt.

Their lips met again in a hungry kiss. Simone's fingers skimmed along his waistband.

His heart thundered in his chest. This moment, this coupling, felt different than the other times they'd made love. Weightier, more poignant somehow.

Simone unbuttoned his slacks and he stepped out of them quickly. He watched as she shed what remained of her clothes, his desperation to be skin to skin growing with each move she made.

He slid a hand along the curve of her hip up to her breast.

Simone let out a little mewl. He walked her backward and they fell onto the bed in a tangle of limbs.

He skimmed his lips over her neck and collarbone, then felt her shift under him and stoke the flames of his growing passion.

She found his mouth in a mix of tenderness and desire.

Their hands and lips roamed each other's bodies. He loved touching her and feeling what her touch did to him.

Finally, when he was sure he couldn't stand another moment, he moved into her.

They moved together in a sensual intimate dance, spiraling toward the total loss of control that they both so desperately wanted.

Afterward, with Simone sleeping in his arms, their hearts beating in a shared rhythm, he didn't want the moment to ever end.

But not a minute after the thought crossed his mind, he heard a buzzing. He slid from the bed and grabbed his phone from the pocket of his pants.

"Webb here," he whispered.

"Sheriff, I think you'd better come to the employee parking lot at city hall right away."

The tone of Deputy Bridges's voice had him shrugging into his pants quickly. "What's going on?"

"We've got another body. And another skull card."

Lance bit back a swear.

"It's bad, Sheriff. The vic? It's Melinda Hanes."

Chapter Twenty-One

A fog as heavy as the rain clouds threatening overhead hung over the scene in the parking lot behind City Hall. Lance's stomach churned with a mixture of anger and despondency. He'd been working nonstop in the hopes of catching the killer before he struck again. And he'd failed. Now it appeared that the killer had taken another woman's life.

He ducked under the crime scene tape and headed for Bridges, who was standing feet away from the body of a woman sprawled on the pavement next to a black sedan. As he got closer, he could see clearly that the woman was Melinda Hanes. Her head was turned to face him, her eyes open wide as if she couldn't believe what had happened.

"Damn," he said when he reached Bridges's side.

"Yeah, this is going to bring a firestorm."

Lance went down on his haunches. "Marks around the neck look like those on Holly Moyer."

"Yep," Bridges agreed. "And we've got this." He lifted the side of Melinda's suit jacket. A playing card with a skull design rested against Melinda's torso.

"Ego." Her card read.

He examined the body closely. Two of the nails on her right hand were broken.

"Looks like she fought her killer." He pointed to the broken nails. "We might be able to get some DNA."

The look Bridges gave him conveyed his skepticism. "Let's hope. Nothing from Holly's body. Looks like he wore gloves."

Lance stood. "Well, let's hope he forgot them this time."

Over Bridges's shoulder, he saw Barber arrive.

"I came as soon as I heard." Barber set his tool kit down next to his feet. "I don't think I really believed that the victim was Melinda Hanes until right this minute."

Lance understood. It didn't seem possible. In a big city, the mayor might have had protection of some sort or at least be surrounded at most times by an entourage. But in Carling Lake it wasn't unusual to see Melinda out and about, shopping on Main Street, catching a bite at Rosie's diner or going for a jog. And that feeling of safety had made it easy for the killer to target her.

"Bridges, let's pull the security video for the building."

"Ah, I can help you there."

Lance turned to see a short woman with a mop of curly brunette hair dressed in a blue uniform. The word *security* was stitched over her left breast pocket.

"Or actually, I can't help you," she added with a cringe.

Lance stepped closer to the woman. "And who are you?"

"My name is Emma Webster. I'm the night supervisor for security at City Hall."

"And what did you mean you can't help us? We'll need that video."

"And I'd turn it over to you if we had it, but cameras facing this area of the parking lot were vandalized a couple of nights ago. I'm sure you know how slow the city requisition department is, Sheriff. The cameras haven't been fixed yet."

Lance fought back the urge to swear.

He got the details of the vandalism from Emma Webster, then cut her loose.

"You think the vandalism is connected to the murder?" Bridges asked.

"Let's check it out. It's too convenient to be a coincidence."

"Will do." Bridges hesitated. "One thing doesn't make sense. Even if our killer disabled the security cameras, how could he be sure when Melinda would leave the building and that she'd be alone when she did?"

"He could have lured her out here when he knew they'd be the only two in the parking lot. We still don't know why Holly Moyer was in Carling Lake, but since we haven't found any connection to the town combing through her life, we can assume she was lured by the killer somehow too."

"Now what?"

"Now we do our jobs. Collect evidence. Have forensics put a rush on the results. We have maybe two hours tops before the entire town council is in my office demanding answers."

Lance's phone buzzed. He pulled it free of his pocket expecting to see a message from one of the aforementioned council members, but the message was from Simone.

She was at the front of City Hall and her message said she needed to talk to him right away but the deputy at the perimeter wasn't letting her pass.

He headed for the front of the building. Simone stood with James.

"You shouldn't be here," he said, frowning when he reached them.

"I tried talking her out of coming down here, but she was insistent. I figured it was best to tag along," James said.

"There's something you need to see." Simone pulled her phone from her purse with a shaky hand.

He took a good look at her face and saw that she was scared. "What is it?"

She flipped the phone so he could see it. James shifted so he could get a look at the screen as well.

YOU DIDN'T LISTEN. YOU'RE NEXT.

He checked the time stamp on the text. It had been sent less than fifteen minutes earlier.

The killer was thumbing his nose at them. Killing Melinda and sending another, far more direct, threatening message to Simone. He was terrified for her.

He scanned the crowd, sizing up the people milling around. No one looked suspicious, but their killer would have to be adept at blending in to have stayed under the radar for so many years.

"Lance, is Melinda dead?" Simone asked in a shaky voice.

The Carling Lake gossip mill was 24/7.

He nodded briskly. "Unfortunately, yes. We found her in the employee parking lot."

She covered her mouth with her hand. "Oh, my God."

"Listen, you need to go back to the B and B with James and stay there, okay?"

As a sign of just how scared she was, Simone nodded. "Okay."

He shot a look at James.

"I've got her. You do what you need to do."

James led Simone to his car. Lance got back to work.

The exterior lights on the building and in the parking lot came on, illuminating the area. A light drizzle began as Barber began removing Melinda's body. Lance turned his attention to processing the crime scene. Without the security footage of the parking lot, they were at a disadvantage, but he'd sent Emma Webster inside with Deputy Bridges to pull whatever footage City Hall did have over the last twenty-four hours. Maybe they'd get lucky and catch the killer coming to or leaving the scene. Carling Lake didn't have traffic cameras at every intersection like some cities and towns, but he'd also have the footage from the cameras they did have pulled. He wanted to catch this killer badly.

He sorted through Melinda's purse with nitrile gloves covering his hands. The wallet inside held three credit cards, her driver's license and fifty dollars. The interior of the purse also contained a small makeup bag, a pack of tissues, half a dozen old receipts, four pens, a key ring and Melinda's city employee badge. The contents appeared to be pretty typical except for the lack of a cell phone. Maybe she'd left it in her office. Or maybe the killer had taken it.

"Be on the lookout for her phone. It's not in her purse," he called out to the men and women processing the scene with him.

"Sheriff, I think I've got something here," Silver, the evidence tech from Holly Moyer's crime scene, called from the other side of Melinda's car.

Lance rounded the car.

Silver was on his hands and knees. He pulled out a cell phone. "Think we've found her phone."

Lance took the phone. The lock screen popped up, barring them from plumbing the phone's secrets. He'd have to leave it with the forensic IT people to open and who knows how long that might take. This case was getting more frustrating by the minute.

"Let me through! Let me through!" A young woman in jeans and a worn T-shirt tried to push past the deputy at the perimeter of the parking lot.

Lance slid Melinda's phone into a plastic evidence bag, then made his way over to the woman.

"Sheriff Webb, is it true? Is Melinda dead?"

"I'm sorry. We have no comment at this time."

"Please, I'm Lupe Ramirez, the mayor's assistant." Tears shimmered in her eyes.

His heart dropped. This was the worst part of his job. "Ms. Ramirez, I'm so very sorry, but Ms. Hanes is dead."

The woman froze for a moment, then let out a sharp keening sound that morphed into a wail. He caught her before she fell to the pavement and held her up through the wave of tears. After several minutes, she'd pulled herself together enough to speak.

"How... What happened?"

"I really can't say at the moment. It would be really helpful if you could answer some questions for me."

She sniffled but nodded.

"When was the last time you saw Ms. Hanes?"

Lupe sniffed again. "Last night. Melinda let me go just before nine."

"Did you leave together?"

"No. Melinda had a few more calls she wanted to make."

"At nine at night?"

"Campaign calls. No rest for the wicked and all that."

"Has Ms. Hanes received any threats? Any confrontations?"

"Melinda always has people who are upset with her for some reason. We have one or two constituents come in every week complaining about something or other. But nothing out of the ordinary happened."

"What about anyone strange or suspicious hanging around?"

"No one." Tears began falling from Lupe's eyes again.

"Okay, Ms. Ramirez, one more question. Do you know the lock code on Ms. Hanes's phone?"

"Yes. It's 11-23-0. November 23. Her mother's birthday."

Lance punched the code into the phone and the home screen sprang to life. "Thank you."

Lupe walked away. Lance headed back to the car and the primary crime scene.

Bridges met him halfway. "I've got the footage from the exterior cameras that are working."

"Good. Melinda's assistant was here. She gave me the password for Melinda's phone."

He shifted through her texts. One, in particular, caught his eye. It was from a number with no name attached and had come in at 9:21 p.m. the night before.

I'M HERE.

There was no context. No other texts in the chain or calls from that number to indicate who the text had come from. But it did suggest that Melinda had planned a meetup with someone last night after her assistant had gone. Maybe she'd used her work phone? Or maybe she and the mystery texter had arranged the meeting in person at some earlier point in time.

Lance was starting to build a picture of Melinda's last minutes of life. She and Lupe had stayed late to work. Around 9:00 p.m. Melinda let Lupe go home, possibly because she was meeting the mystery texter. Lupe left and twenty minutes later Melinda received the text from whoever she'd planned to meet saying he'd arrived. She went to the parking lot and the mystery texter killed her.

Which meant Melinda Hanes knew the serial killer even if she didn't know he was a serial killer.

"Bridges. Call this number in to the station. See if they can tell us who it belongs to." He moved away from Melinda's texting app to her email app. She had three separate accounts, one personal, one official and a third for her campaign. He scrolled through the inbox for the campaign address. There were thousands of messages, most unopened. But among the messages that had been read was one from Zane Goodman Web Design. He searched Zane Goodman Web Design in the app. The search returned several dozen messages. Opening up one of the earliest messages, he learned that Zane had set up Melinda's campaign website.

A familiar flutter started in his stomach. Zane Goodman had contact with all three of his victims. Holly Moyer and Melinda Hanes through his work and Kate Morelli through the *Carling Lake Weekly*.

But Zane would have been eighteen or nineteen at the time of the first three Card Killer murders. That was outside the age range on the profile the state police had worked up. Other parts of the profile didn't fit, at least not that Lance knew, but based on the police file on the case, Zane Goodman had never been considered a suspect, so there were a lot of unknowns about him. One thing was a given. Even if he wasn't the original Card Killer, growing up in Carling Lake during the time of the original murders, he could have known everything he needed to commit copycat murders.

"Bridges," he called. Bridges lowered his phone from his ear. "We need to bring Zane Goodman in now. And get a search warrant for his home, vehicle and electronics."

"On it. That number you gave me comes back to a burner phone," Bridges said.

"A burner phone in Carling Lake. Can't be but a few places where you can buy one of those. Run it down."

"Yes, sir."

If Zane was a murderer, Lance was going to make sure he never hurt another soul.

Chapter Twenty-Two

Simone wasn't surprised when Lance didn't make it back to the B and B by breakfast. He was bound to have a circus on his hands with the murder of the mayor. She'd spent most of the night working herself, gathering as much information as she could on Clare Davenport. Thankfully, Carling Lake High had digitized its old yearbooks, so she'd been able to match a face to a social media page for the woman she was pretty sure had been Nancy Oliver's best friend. But with Lance dealing with the investigation into the attack on Kate as well as a new murder, who knew when he'd have time to follow up on speaking to Clare.

In her gut, Simone knew they were getting close to the answers that would bring justice to the Card Killer's victims. She just had to keep pushing forward even if it meant breaking her promise to Lance not to go off alone.

She finished a short piece with what she had on Melinda's death for the *Weekly*'s website and let Aaron know that she was going to talk to Clare before heading into the office.

The Davenports lived in a modest two-story town-home in Branford, about an hour north of Carling Lake.

Simone noted the blue minivan parked in one of the two spaces reserved for the Davenport address as she pulled into a visitor's spot. A jump rope and one roller skate lay abandoned in the postage stamp–sized front yard, marking the home as one with children.

She rang the doorbell and waited. No sound came from within. She hadn't called before making the drive, figuring it was better to beg forgiveness than to ask permission or something like that. That was starting to look like a miscalculation. She rang the doorbell again and peered through the vertical window next to the door. The house remained quiet.

Clare Davenport's Facebook page gave her occupation as a homemaker and several of the photographs on social media had included shots of the van parked in front of the house now, indicating it was Clare's primary vehicle. So where was she?

A child's wail sounded from behind her. Simone turned, locking on to the source of the sound. A child sat on the wood chip–covered playground at the far end of the parking lot cradling his leg. A harried-looking woman with her red hair thrown into a messy bun at the top of her head squatted next to him. Three other women stood nearby, their attention moving back and forth between the children still playing on the equipment and the mother and child at their feet.

Simone headed toward the playground. A slim blonde wearing the same tortoiseshell glasses from

Clare Davenport's social media pages turned and watched her approach. The look in her eye was wary, making Simone wonder if she wasn't the first reporter to approach Clare Davenport recently.

"Clare Davenport?"

The two other women standing with Clare turned, sizing up Simone. Clare took a step away from them.

"Yes. May I ask who is inquiring?" Her tone was cautious and Simone thought she detected a hint of fear.

She smiled in an attempt to put the woman at ease.

"My name is Simone Jarrett. I was hoping I could have a word with you."

Clare glanced at her friends. "About what?"

This was the tricky part, or one of the tricky parts. Asking the questions she wanted to ask about Nancy in front of the other mothers was unlikely to produce the answers Simone wanted.

"It will just take a minute. We could go over there so you can still keep an eye on the kids." Simone pointed to a bench several feet away, out of earshot of the other mothers.

Clare glanced again at the other women, who were now openly watching their conversation.

Simone could sense she was on the verge of being turned down.

"Please. I promise I'll just take a moment of your time."

Clare hesitated for a moment longer before nodding.

They walked together to the bench.

"You're a reporter, right?" Clare asked as soon as they'd sat.

"I am. For the *Carling Lake Weekly.*"

"Every few years I get a phone call or email from a reporter doing a story on the Card Killer. This year I've gotten several. I guess because it's been twenty years now and no one has been able to catch the monster. Why you people find that fascinating, I'll never understand."

"I don't find it fascinating. I find it sad. I find it to be an affront to justice."

A look of surprise flashed in Clare's eyes. She peered at Simone for a long moment. "I believe you do." Clare turned and watched the kids playing.

"I am doing a story profiling the lives of the women who were murdered by the Card Killer. But you might have heard there has been a murder in Carling Lake that resemble the murders from twenty years ago."

Lance hadn't publicly connected Melinda's murder to the Card Killer but the text she'd received after Melinda's body was found left no doubt about the connection.

Clare sucked in a sharp breath. "I hadn't heard. My parents moved to Florida years ago and I don't keep up with anyone in Carling Lake anymore."

"The sheriff is investigating the connection and I'm trying to help by digging up any information that I can."

"What did you want to ask me?"

"I spoke to Wendall Oliver. He said you and his daughter, Nancy, were close?"

A ghost of a smile crossed Clare's face. "Mr. Oliver was such a nice man. Nancy gave him hell after her mother died." She turned so she faced Simone. "Nancy and I were close. My family lived next door to her family. Went all the way from kindergarten through the twelfth grade together."

"You don't hear about a lot of childhood friendships lasting that long."

"I always wondered whether we'd have been friends under different circumstances. Like, if we hadn't lived next door to each other and our parents hadn't been friends. If we'd just been two of the hundred girls who went to the same school, would we have been best friends?"

"I guess those are the kinds of what-ifs we all ask ourselves sometimes."

"I guess." Clare glanced at the playground.

Simone followed her gaze. There were seven or eight kids all elementary school age or younger running around. She wasn't sure which two were Clare's. There were a ton of photos of her kids on her social media pages, but the best Simone could make out from the raging, wailing bodies on the playground in front of her was that the ones with brunette hair weren't Clare's. Her two boys had golden-blond hair and piercing blue eyes just like their mother.

"Nancy and I were best friends, but we couldn't have been more different. I was a rule follower. Studious and maybe a bit too serious for a kid. Nancy never met a rule she didn't want to break. Even when her mother was alive, she pushed the boundaries of what she could get away with."

"When did her mother die?"

"When we were fourteen. A terrible time for a child to lose a parent. Not that there's a great time," she added quickly. "Kids are going through so much at that age, and to add something like the death of a parent on top of adolescence, well, it's not easy."

"I understand what you mean."

"For Nancy, it was like losing her mother ripped away any inhibitions she had. She started skipping school. Hanging out with an older crowd. Drinking. Smoking weed. We stayed friends during high school, but we weren't nearly as close as we'd been."

A bloodcurdling scream came from the direction of the large slide. Simone started, but Clare didn't even look over. The other moms didn't move from their places either. Apparently, it was nothing to worry about, so Simone carried on with her questions.

"Were you still friends at the time of her death?"

"Friendly, I'd say. We'd hang out when I was home from college. I went away. Nancy barely made it out of high school, so she hung around Carling Lake taking whatever job she could find."

"Her father told me she wanted to be a dancer."

Clare chuckled ruefully. "I guess so, but like in that way that you know she's never going to achieve it. Nancy liked having a dream more than she liked working to make that dream a reality, you know what I mean?"

"I do. But she was working at The Palace Theater?"

Clare rolled her eyes. "Yeah. Sounds classy. At least classy enough to fool her father at first. When he found out, he lost it."

That was consistent with what Mr. Oliver had told her and Lance, but there was still the question of Nancy's possible boyfriend.

"Nancy's father said she had a boyfriend?" Simone pressed.

The little boy who'd been crying on the ground when she'd approached the park ran by, chasing a girl in pigtails with a stick. His red-haired mother yelled at him to put the stick down and play nicely.

Clare's gaze tracked the children. "We went out that night, me and Nancy," she said, ignoring the question.

Her voice was little more than a whisper, but it rang like a bell in Simone's head.

"The night Nancy was killed? You were with her?" Simone asked.

Clare nodded. She shifted her gaze back to the kids on the playground equipment, but it was as if she was looking through them back into the past.

"I was home for the weekend with my college boyfriend. Nancy suggested we go out for a drink. None of us was twenty-one yet, but she knew a place that would serve us. I could tell Cory wanted to go. He'd been eyeing Nancy from the moment I introduced them." She laughed without mirth. "I didn't like it and I'll admit I was jealous, but I wanted to be the cool girlfriend so I agreed. We each had a couple of drinks. We were having fun and then I stepped away to the ladies' room."

The kids around them continued to play, but it was as if she and Clare had entered their own little bubble. She could hear the shrieks and laughter, but they sounded muffled, far off. Every cell in her body was focused on Clare and the story she was telling.

"When I got back to the bar, Nancy and Cory weren't there. I walked around the space looking for them, thinking maybe a table had opened up and they'd grabbed it while I was in the bathroom."

"But that's not what happened."

Clare shook her head. "No. I found them in a dark corner. Climbing all over each other."

"What did you do?"

"I pulled them apart. Called Cory every name in the book and told him he'd better be gone by the time I got back to my parents' house. He had enough sense to leave. I'd never been so mad. Then I turned on Nancy after Cory left. It got ugly. We said things… dredged up things from years earlier that had been festering."

"That's not uncommon when longtime friends argue."

"We got out of hand. Nancy slapped me." Clare looked into Simone's eyes. "I have never raised my hand to another living soul, but if some guy in the bar hadn't grabbed me, I would have pummeled Nancy."

Simone let several heartbeats pass before she asked her next question. "Then what happened?"

"I left. I walked home. Cory was gone. My parents were concerned, but I put them off. Told them it was nothing. Nancy and I had argued, but I'd figure it out in the morning."

"But by the morning—"

"Nancy was dead." Clare wiped a tear from her cheek. "I should have walked home with her. Or at least sent her father or my father to the bar to pick her up, but I was so mad."

Simone covered Clare's hand with her own. "You can't blame yourself. The only person to blame is the man who killed Nancy."

Maybe it was because she was on the opposite side of the situation this time. Or maybe it was simply the realization that a lot of people made a lot of decisions that ended with Nancy Oliver being killed one night twenty years ago, including Nancy herself. But when she repeated the words that Lance had said to her, she believed them.

They sat in silence for a moment, giving Clare time to compose herself. Simone had noticed the other moms watching them, but none had approached. Maybe it was mother's instinct, but they seemed to get that Clare wasn't in any danger and that whatever was going on was emotionally weighty.

Several minutes later Clare had composed herself once again.

"You never answered my question about Nancy's boyfriend. Do you know who he was?" Simone asked softly.

Clare looked at her. "I don't know for sure."

"But you suspect?"

Clare let out a deep breath. "I don't want to get anyone in trouble. Especially not such a nice guy."

Simone's heart rate ticked up. "No one except the killer is going to get in trouble, but the sheriff needs to question anyone who may know anything that can help him find the killer."

"Of course, you're right. One of the times I came home from school before Nancy really went wild, I dropped by Nancy's place to see if she wanted to hang out. I rang the bell and no one came to the door, but I could hear the television playing and someone inside. When I looked through the front window into the living room, I saw Nancy on the couch going at it with Zane Goodman."

Chapter Twenty-Three

Lance walked into the interrogation room with a folder and the bag with Melinda's phone tucked under his arm. He sat in the chair across from Zane and opened the folder, placing eight by ten photos of Holly, Kate and Melinda side by side facing Zane.

Zane looked at each photograph, then glanced across the table at Lance. "What is this?"

"You tell me. Each of these women has been attacked by the same man. Two are dead. One is in the hospital fighting for her life. The only thing we can find that they have in common is you."

"Me?" Zane's voice went up an octave. "No way. No way." He pushed the photos away. "I didn't have anything to do with what happened to those women."

"Okay, then tell me where you were the night Holly was murdered."

Zane took Lance through what he'd done the night of Holly Moyer's death, the day Kate was attacked and the previous night when Melinda Hanes was killed. His alibi for each attack was weak. He'd been home alone at every relevant time. Not unusual for a man who lived alone, but not convincing either.

"What do you know about the Card Killer case?" Lance asked.

"I know what I read in the paper. What the rumor mill said when the attacks occurred, although I was just a kid back then, so I'm sure my parents kept a lot of it from me."

"You were nineteen when the first three murders took place. Hardly a kid."

"Look, at nineteen, all I wanted to do was get out of this town. I didn't even know those women."

Lance tapped the photos of Holly, Kate and Melinda on the table. "Maybe not, but you knew these women."

Zane's face paled, but his voice never lost its bravado. "Barely. I mean, I already told you I did work for the resort Holly worked at, but I only met her a couple of times. And everyone in town knew Melinda Hanes. She's the mayor. And Kate, she's just my dad's intern. I don't think I said more than 'good morning' and 'have a good evening' to her in the time she's been working at the paper."

If Zane was a serial killer, he wouldn't break easily. He'd gotten away with murder for twenty years. He probably felt like he was smarter than law enforcement. Lance would have to turn up the heat on Zane if he wanted to get anywhere.

"Why did you leave Carling Lake twenty years ago?"

"Why did I… I was barely more than a kid when I left for college."

Lance shook his head. "No, see, I looked into it. After high school, you worked for a year at the *Weekly* while taking classes in Stunnersville. Then all of a sudden you went away to school. All the way to Seattle. Right after Nancy Oliver's murder."

Zane's eyes shifted to the wall behind Lance's head and his knee bounced to a silent beat. He was hiding something.

"Zane, I'm going to find out. It will be better for you if you come clean. Did you know Nancy Oliver?"

He swallowed. "I… No."

A lie. But Lance couldn't prove it was a lie, not yet, so he switched tactics. "You're good with computers, I understand. Do you also know anything about security cameras?"

Confusion clouded Zane's face. "What? I know how to build web pages, but that doesn't make me a computer wizard or anything. And I don't know the first thing about security cameras."

Lance pointed across the table. "You see, I do believe you are telling me the truth there. Because whoever attacked Melinda Hanes last night thought they'd disabled the security cameras facing the parking lot, but you know these computer guys, they can work wonders. They tell me that it will take a little time but that they can recover the footage."

It was a lie, but Zane didn't know that. If he thought they had him on tape committing murder, maybe that would be enough to get him to confess.

Zane shrugged. "Good. Then you'll see I didn't kill anyone."

Or maybe not.

Lance slid the plastic bag with Melinda's phone toward Zane. "Do you recognize this?"

Zane's brow furrowed. "It's a phone. Should I know more about it than that?"

"It's Melinda Hanes's phone. Last night she got a text from someone luring her to the parking lot where she was killed. Know anything about that?"

Zane slammed his hands down on the table. "I already told you. I don't know anything about any murders."

Lance kept his voice even. "Calm down, Mr. Goodman. I'm just asking questions here. If you're innocent, you have nothing to worry about."

Zane glared.

Lance waited a beat before asking his next question. "Do you recognize this phone number?" He read off the number the text to Melinda had come from.

"No," Zane said through clenched teeth.

"Do you own a burner phone?"

"No."

"Have you ever owned or bought a burner phone?"

Zane shifted in his chair, visibly uncomfortable. "I don't know. Maybe."

"What for?"

"What for?"

"Why did you buy a burner?"

"I told you, I don't know if I did. You asked me if I ever owned or bought a burner. I may have at some point in the past but not recently."

Lance stood and walked to the side of the table

where Zane sat. He leaned over the man, crowding into his space. "I'm going to get a warrant to search your home. What am I going to find there, Zane?"

Zane leaned away as far as he could without falling off his chair. "Nothing. The usual stuff people keep in their homes."

"No thin pieces of wire you've been using to wrap around women's necks, choking the life out of them? Or how about playing cards with a skull design on them?"

Zane glowered. "I'm done talking. I want a lawyer."

Lance straightened, shooting the man a glare of his own. "Fine. You want to play it that way? So be it."

A knock came on the door. Deputy Bridges poked his head into the room. "Sheriff, can I talk to you for a minute?"

Lance grabbed Melinda's cell phone but left the photos in the room with Zane and stepped out into the hallway.

"I was able to find out where the burner phone was purchased," Bridges said.

Lance was impressed. "That was quick work."

Bridges smiled. "You were right about there only being a few places to purchase a burner in Carling Lake. And I got lucky in the first place. Wright's Pharmacy."

Lance's internal antenna went up. There were rarely coincidences in police work. Wright's Pharmacy showing up again probably wasn't going to be the exception to that rule.

"Was Zane Goodman the purchaser? I could use something concrete to throw at him."

Bridges shook his head. "Not Zane. Aaron."

Chapter Twenty-Four

Zane was the Card Killer.

Simone had left Clare to care for her kids and was in the car headed back to Carling Lake. Her head spun, but it made sense. Zane had been dating Nancy at the time of her murder. They both must have worked hard to keep it a secret. She knew firsthand how much the residents of her adopted town loved gossip of the romantic variety and she doubted that had changed over the years. Maybe Zane had pressured Nancy to keep their relationship a secret. Simone knew serial killers were good at convincing people to do what they wanted. It was one of the reasons they were able to fly under the radar so well. That and they seemed so normal. She couldn't say that she liked Zane very much, but she definitely wouldn't have pegged him for a killer. Which also fit the profile.

Zane also had a connection to Juanita Byers, although that one was much more tenuous. Juanita had interviewed with his parents for a job. Maybe Zane met her then. Or maybe he knew her through her job at Wright's Pharmacy. As a resident of Carling Lake, he'd probably been in the store any number of times. And Deborah Indigo? She couldn't think of a connection between Zane and Deborah, but that didn't mean there wasn't one. Deborah had been a housewife, and if memory served, Deborah had several kids. Maybe one of them was a friend of Zane's or had gone to school with him. There was a connection. Her reporter's instinct was humming with it.

One thing she knew without a doubt was that Zane had connections to all three of the women who'd been killed or attacked in the last several days. He knew Kate from the *Weekly*. He'd worked with Holly on the Fairmont's website, and everyone knew Melinda. Melinda made sure of that.

Simone wouldn't be surprised if there was a closer connection between them as well. Now that she knew who to look at, she'd keep digging until she found it.

The rain had held off until she'd gotten back on the road to Carling Lake, but it was coming down hard now. She was about halfway back to town, on a stretch of the two-lane highway that was sandwiched between a large swath of open land on one side and a swampy marsh on the other. Headlights flashed through the rain behind her. She couldn't make out the model of the car, but given how high the headlights were, it had to be an SUV of some type. And it was moving dangerously fast.

"Idiot."

She kept an eye on the rearview mirror. Unease stirred in her stomach. Hopefully, the maniac would just go around.

The other car was close now. Close enough that she could see that it was an Escalade. One that looked a lot like the Escalade that had driven her and Lance off the road.

She sped up.

So did the SUV.

She was already going well over the speed limit, perilously fast given the weather, but she pushed the gas pedal to the floor anyway.

The 4Runner shot forward and so did the Escalade behind her.

She had to do something. Get help.

Despite the danger of it, she reached across the console for her phone. Using the voice commands, she ordered the phone to dial Lance.

While it rang, she prayed for him to answer.

"Simone, now is not a good time—"

"The Escalade from the other day, it's chasing me right now."

"Where are you?" Lance barked.

"Route 7. Between Branford and Carling Lake. I talked to Clare Davenport. She said that Nancy was dating Zane Goodman not long before she died. Zane must be driving the Escalade. He's the Card Killer."

"Simone, hang on. I'm letting Highway Patrol know and I'm on my way."

"Did you hear me? I think Zane's the Card Killer."

"It's not Zane, Simone. Zane is in an interrogation room at the sheriff's department."

Simone was stunned. If Zane wasn't chasing her, who was?

She didn't have any more time to contemplate the question. The Escalade roared and slammed into the back of the 4Runner.

The car hydroplaned, sailing across the highway into the lane going in the opposite direction.

Her scream reverberated around the interior of the car.

She let up on the accelerator and jerked the car back into the proper lane.

Her heart thundered in her chest.

"Simone! Are you still there?" Lance's frantic voice came from the phone, which had fallen to the floor on the passenger side of the 4Runner.

"I'm here," she yelled. "The Escalade just rammed me."

There was nowhere to go. No side roads or homes along the highway. Not even other cars that might see what was going on and call for help. The rain must have been keeping people inside and off the highway.

Everyone except the driver of the Escalade.

With another roar of its engine, the Escalade slammed into the back of her car again. This time the 4Runner spun. Once. Twice. Three times, completely disorienting her.

The car finally stopped spinning, thankfully facing in the right direction. She pressed down on the accelerator, but she didn't get far before the Escalade hit her again. For a moment it felt as if she was floating. Then her head slammed against the steering wheel before snapping back against the headrest. The world spun. Grass and sky. Sky and grass. She could no longer tell which way was up. In some part of her mind, she realized the 4Runner had flipped. More than once. But her body seemed to have gone into protective mode. She knew what was happening, but it felt as if she was seeing it from outside her body.

The 4Runner finally came to a stop with a shudder that vibrated through her body.

And then there was nothing but darkness.

It took an effort to open her eyes. A wave of pain smashed into her along with consciousness. Every part of her body hurt, but a searing pain shot through her shoulder and she hung upside down.

It took a moment, but the 4Runner flipping and all that had led up to it came rushing back to her. Where was the Escalade's driver now? Was she still in danger? She couldn't just stay there. She had to hide.

The airbag had inflated, probably saving her life. She slapped it away, then screamed with the pain that shot up her arm and back.

Okay, so her right shoulder had most likely been dislocated. She was able to unfasten her seat belt with her left hand. She dropped to the roof of the car, jerking her shoulder again. She whimpered, the pain nearly blinding. But she didn't have time to wallow.

The driver's-side window had shattered in the rollover. Wind had joined the rain, sending it falling sideways and into the car.

Simone crawled through the glass, adding small cuts to her hands to her list of injuries.

The 4Runner had found its final resting place in

the swampy marsh along the side of the road. She crawled through the mud and muck. In seconds she was not only drenched but filthy. Mud seeped through her slacks and made its way up the sleeves of her shirt.

She crawled a few feet from the car, panting heavily from the effort it took to move her body. She glanced at the road. The Escalade was nowhere to be seen, but that didn't mean much. A curtain of rain fell, obscuring everything more than a few feet away.

If the Escalade's driver was still out there, she needed to get as far away from the 4Runner as possible.

She pushed to her knees and then, shakily, to her feet. The pain of doing so was so intense she had to fight back the urge to scream.

Hot tears mingled with ice-cold raindrops on her face.

Through the rain and tears, she saw a beam of light. Someone was there with a flashlight.

Help?

But the tentacles of fear snaking up her spine warned that the source of the light did not want to find her to help her.

Buoyed by fear, she moved as fast as she could, knowing it wasn't fast enough.

"Simone! Come out, come out wherever you are!"

Even with the sound of the rain and wind, the voice was unmistakable.

Aaron.

Not Zane.

Aaron was the Card Killer.

A rush of adrenaline spurred her on. The rain and muck made it impossible to see where she was going, but it also shielded her from sight and muffled the sound of her movements. If she could put enough distance between herself and Aaron, maybe she could get to the street and flag down a passing motorist.

The pain in her shoulder screamed, but she pressed on.

"Come on now, Simone. It's cold and wet out here. Whatever you're thinking, you'll never make it. Give up now and I'll kill you quickly."

She was in so much pain that for just a moment she thought about doing just that. But she stayed silent. She felt like she was dying, but she didn't want to die.

A new sound cut through the pouring rain. A siren.

"Damn it," Aaron swore, his voice coming from far closer than she'd have liked.

And then suddenly he was in front of her. Holding a gun.

"There you are."

He grabbed her arm, wrenching her shoulder further from its socket.

She couldn't hold back the scream of pain.

"Simone! Where are you?" Lance cried out.

"It's Aaron. He has a gun!"

Aaron aimed a spray of gunfire in the direction that Lance's voice had come from.

She did her best to break free of his hold, but Aaron's grip was firm.

"Why, Aaron?"

"Why?" He pulled her farther into the swamp.

"Because nobody else would. Those women, all of them were blights on this community. Thieves. Egotists. Harlots. Busybodies. Crooks. All of them."

Her best bet now was to keep him talking long enough for Lance to find them. "How do you know that? You don't get to play judge and jury."

Aaron pulled her forward. "How do I know? Deborah Indigo. My first kill. Deborah and I had an affair. Something just for fun, but she let it go to her head. Started pressuring me to leave Margaret. And Nancy, she was corrupting my boy."

"And Juanita?" Simone shouted over the rain.

"She had some nerve coming to me for a job after stealing from Wright. Brazen."

"But she didn't steal the money. You said you believed her."

"So she says. I knew the moment she came into my office what I had to do. I called her that night. Told her she got the job and that I needed her to start early the next morning but that I had a meeting, so I'd need her to come in and do the paperwork that night. She was so happy to have a job she didn't even question the timing."

Simone was revolted by the smugness she heard in his tone. He'd preyed on Juanita's desperation in order to kill her and he hadn't felt a moment of guilt or concern about it.

"And the more recent women?"

"You're all the same. Zane heard the rumors about Holly and the manager. He told me all about her. Melinda, well, everyone knew how corrupt she and her family were."

"And Kate?"

"That's your fault. I tried to warn you away from pursuing the story. You wouldn't give it up. Even after I broke into your house. I didn't know how much she knew, so she had to go." Aaron pushed her forward and pointed the gun at her chest. "Just like you."

"Lance knows you're the Card Killer. Killing me won't stop him from arresting you."

"Maybe not. But I'm going to do it anyway."

Her body tensed and she closed her eyes.

The sound of the gunshot blared around the swamp.

It took her a moment to realize she hadn't been shot.

She opened her eyes to see Lance standing over Aaron's body. Lance kicked the gun from Aaron's hand, flipped him onto his stomach and cuffed him behind his back.

A second later he was at Simone's side. She fell against him, her last bit of energy spent.

Lance wrapped his arms around her, holding her up.

"We did it. We caught him," she said, consciousness fading fast.

The last thing she heard before the darkness claimed her was "You caught him, sweetheart. *You* did it."

Chapter Twenty-Five

Simone woke to blinding lights and an incessant beeping that immediately signaled she was in the hospital.

Her vision was blurred, but she made out Lance sitting slumped over in the chair next to the hospital bed.

"Lance?"

"Hey." Relief spread across his handsome face. He scooted closer and pressed his mouth to hers with such gentleness that for the moment she could forget where she was and how she'd gotten there.

He broke off the kiss, but instead of pulling back he rested his forehead against hers. "You gave me one hell of a scare."

"I gave myself one too," she answered wryly. She let her hands linger on his stubble-covered cheeks. "Are you okay?"

He chuckled, pulling away and sitting on the edge of the bed. "Am I okay? You're the one in the hospital bed."

"You were shot at."

"I'm fine, sweetheart. Don't worry about me."

She attempted to sit up.

"Hey, take it easy." He helped her shift slowly into a more upright position.

Her limbs felt as if they were made of lead while her thoughts swam in a fog of cotton.

"How long have I been out?" She croaked.

Lance reached for the pitcher on the table at the foot of the bed. He poured water into the cup and held it to her lips. "The doctors gave you a sedative. You've been out for a few hours. You've got a mild concussion and a few scrapes and bruises. You'll likely be sore for a few days, but thankfully there was no permanent damage."

She took a sip, then he set the cup aside.

"Is this a good time for a visit?" Erika hovered in the doorway to the hospital room, James behind her. He carried a bouquet of roses and Erika clutched a clear plastic container full of chocolate chip cookies.

"Absolutely."

Erika rushed into the room, handing the cookies off to Lance and throwing her arms around Simone.

"Oh, sorry." Erika pulled back, concern lacing her eyes. "I didn't hurt you, did I?"

"No. I'm fine. A little banged up, but nothing serious."

"I'm so glad. I can't believe what you've been through. The accident. Aaron's role in everything. It's like a bad movie."

She wished it was fiction. But it wasn't. This was reality and the reality was her friend and boss was a serial killer.

"What about Aaron?" Just saying her boss's name sent a spike of fear through her chest. The machine she was currently hooked up to blinked and beeped, reflecting the uptick in her pulse.

Lance's expression turned hard. "You don't have to worry about him." He squeezed her hand. "The doctors were able to save his life, but he'll be spending the rest of it in a jail cell. I'll make sure of that."

"I heard the state police are questioning Margaret and Zane," James said.

Simone's heart jumped into her throat. "Were they involved in the murders too?"

"Not as far as we know," Lance responded. "I didn't want to leave you, so I called the state police. They'll look into every possibility. If there's anyone else involved, we'll find out. They'll want to talk to you also."

"Aaron admitted to killing Deborah, Juanita, Holly, Melinda and Nancy," Simone said. "He and Deborah were having an affair and she was pushing him to leave Margaret. He said he killed her."

"What about all the other women? He couldn't have been having affairs with all of them," Erika said, disgust lacing her tone.

Simone shook her head. "No. After killing Deborah, it seems like he saw himself as some kind of vigilante. Punishing women he felt had done wrong. He knew Juanita had been fired by Harry Wright for stealing and he was incensed that she'd applied to the *Weekly*. And he knew that Zane was seeing Nancy, who he didn't think was the kind of woman his son should be cavorting with. His words, not mine. Is that why he killed Holly? Was Zane the mystery boyfriend Arianna told us about?" Simone asked Lance.

"It doesn't look like it. Again, it's only been a few hours, so we're still piecing the puzzle together, but based on your conversation with Clare Davenport, we think Zane was seeing Nancy twenty years ago. But he wasn't lying about his relationship with Holly being completely professional on his end. Holly asked him out a few times, but he always declined."

Erika's brow furrowed in thought. "So who was the mystery man you guys were looking for?"

"Aaron." The realization hit Simone and she said the name at the same time as Lance.

"It's not clear yet how it started, but we believe Aaron and Holly began an affair at some point," Lance said. "The calls to the burner phone that Aaron bought and Holly's tales about her well-off secret boyfriend lean that way. We think the affair and Holly getting pregnant was the trigger for him to start killing again. I'm sure we'll find more evidence as the investigation continues. Hopefully, Aaron will tell us everything he knows once he realizes there's no way out for him."

The four heads in the room turned toward the doorway at the sound of a soft knock.

Kate looked timidly over the group. "I don't mean to interrupt. I just wanted to thank Simone for saving my life."

Simone held both her hands out to Kate. She looked much better than she had the last time Simone had seen her. The color was back in her cheeks and the marks on her neck seemed to have faded some.

Erika, James and Lance made space for Kate to stand at the side of Simone's bed. "You don't have to thank me. I'm so glad I got to your apartment in time."

"Me too. So are my parents. They are waiting in the car, but they say to tell you they are forever in your debt. So am I."

"No. There's no debt here. I did what anyone would have done."

Kate gave her a tight smile. "I'm going back home with them. Now actually. The hospital is going to discharged me today, and, well, with everything that's happened, I think home is where I want to be for a while."

"That's understandable." Simone took the young woman's hand. "When you're ready to look for a job in journalism, call me. References. Introductions. Whatever you need. I think you're going to be a terrific journalist."

Kate's smile was genuine. "Deputy Bridges has your flash drive with the Card Killer files. I told him where to find it. Thank goodness I'd hidden under my bathroom sink."

Simone wasn't sure she ever wanted to see those files again, but she thanked Kate.

A male nurse stepped into the room. "Okay, I didn't say anything when there was one more visitor in this room than there should be, but now there are far too many people in here. Our patient needs her rest."

Kate said a quick goodbye and scurried out of the room. Erika gave her another hug and James planted a chaste kiss on her cheek before leaving.

Lance pulled a chair close to the bed, sat down and crossed one ankle over the other, making it clear he had no intention of leaving.

The nurse rolled his eyes. "The doctor will be in soon for rounds. He'll want to see you, since the sedative has worn off."

"You don't have to stay, you know," she said after the nurse left.

He moved from the chair to sit on the side of the bed. "I'm not going anywhere." After a moment's hesitation, he said, "How about you?"

"What do you mean?"

"This is probably not the right time for this, but who knows what is going to happen with the *Weekly*. Even if Margaret keeps it going or sells it to someone, are you going to want to work there? And if you aren't working at the *Weekly*, does that mean you're going to look for a job in another town? I know finding a salaried job as a reporter isn't easy these days."

"Whoa. Hang on there. Mild concussion here, remember? I don't want to overtax my brain while it's healing itself."

"Sorry, I know it's not the right time. I just...don't want to lose you."

She reached for his hand and met his gaze. "You aren't going to lose me. I don't know what my future holds at the moment, but I do know this. You and Carling Lake are my home. I'm not going anywhere, Sheriff."

The sensors on the machines around her went off again as Lance leaned forward and she sank into a kiss sealing her promise.

* * * * *

Look for more books in K.D. Richards's West Investigations miniseries later this year!

And in case you missed the previous titles in the series:

Pursuit of the Truth
Missing at Christmas
Christmas Data Breach
Shielding Her Son
Dark Water Disappearance

You'll find them wherever Harlequin Intrigue books are sold!

COMING NEXT MONTH FROM

⬡HARLEQUIN

INTRIGUE

YOU CAN FIND MORE INFORMATION ON UPCOMING HARLEQUIN TITLES, FREE EXCERPTS AND MORE AT HARLEQUIN.COM.

HICNM0323

HARLEQUIN
PLUS

Try the best multimedia subscription service for romance readers like you!

Read, Watch and Play.

Experience the easiest way to get the romance content you crave.

Start your **FREE TRIAL** at
<u>www.harlequinplus.com/freetrial</u>.